The pull of the tide was strong, but so was she.

She sloshed out to deeper water and paddled past the sheltered cove. In the distance, the swaying cabbage palms that dotted Isla Marsopa bent under the increasing pressure of the storm. The familiar twinge twisted her gut as she thought about her past with Reuben Sandoval, exploring that tiny paradise.

Keep swimming, she told herself fiercely. Paralleling the shore, she fought the tumbling waves, making her arduous way up the coast, intermittently treading water to preserve her strength. In the distance, she caught sight of the dock where Reuben kept his beloved boat, and for a painful moment, she wondered if he had painted over the name on the stern, *Black-Eyed Beauty,* his nickname for her.

Over the cresting foam, she caught a glimpse of a Jet Ski moving slowly, the driver twisting his head around as if he was looking for something.

Not something. Her nerves sizzled.

Someone.

Her.

Books by Dana Mentink

Love Inspired Suspense

Killer Cargo
Flashover
Race to Rescue
Endless Night
Betrayal in the Badlands
Turbulence
Buried Truth
Escape from the Badlands

*Lost Legacy
*Dangerous Melody
*Final Resort
†Shock Wave
†Force of Nature

*Treasure Seekers
†Stormswept

DANA MENTINK

lives in California, where the weather is golden and the cheese divine. Her family includes two girls (affectionately nicknamed Yogi and Boo Boo). Papa Bear works for the fire department; he met Dana doing a dinner theater production of *The Velveteen Rabbit.* Ironically, their parts were husband and wife.

Dana is a 2009 American Christian Fiction Writers Book of the Year finalist for romantic suspense and an award winner in the Pacific Northwest Writers Literary Contest. Her novel *Betrayal in the Badlands* won a 2010 RT Reviewers' Choice Award. She has enjoyed writing a mystery series for Barbour Books and more than ten novels to date for the Love Inspired Suspense line.

She spent her college years competing in speech and debate tournaments all around the country. Besides writing, she busies herself teaching elementary school and reviewing books for her blog. Mostly, she loves to be home with her family, including a dog with social-anxiety problems, a chubby box turtle and a quirky parakeet.

Dana loves to hear from her readers via her website, at www.danamentink.com.

FORCE OF NATURE
DANA MENTINK

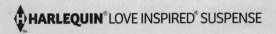
HARLEQUIN® LOVE INSPIRED® SUSPENSE

Recycling programs
for this product may
not exist in your area.

 LOVE INSPIRED BOOKS

ISBN-13: 978-0-373-67586-9

FORCE OF NATURE

He calmed the storm to a whisper
and stilled the waves.
—*Psalms* 107:29

To the brave men and women of the U.S. Coast Guard.
Semper Paratus

ONE

Something about the man silhouetted on the dock made Antonia Verde's body hum with tension. His aviator sunglasses caught the waning Florida sunlight as he peered at his sleek cell phone, his mop of sandy hair tousled around his face by a steady breeze. No different than any other tourist basking in the warmth of a late November afternoon, Antonia told herself, eyeing him from the beach below.

The waves, green-gold and fueled by an approaching storm, slapped at her ankles. The air held a sharp scent of rain, roiling clouds speckling the white sand with shadows. Perhaps it was the threat of inclement weather that made her jumpy. But it was an incoming tropical storm, nothing more, hardly a source of concern for a lifelong Floridian, and she'd wanted a quick sketch of the agitated surf.

More likely her uneasy feelings were a by-product of what she'd recently survived. Having just returned from San Francisco, where she was almost buried alive in an earthquake-ravaged opera house,

she had a right to be jittery. Not to mention the fact
that she'd had the uncanny feeling she'd been followed on her way home from the airport by someone in an expensive car. All she'd seen of him was
a flash of an arm through the partially rolled-down
window, a split-second glimpse of his face. Who
would follow an out-of-work artist driving a beat-
up Ford?

I'm just on edge, that's all.

Memories from her disastrous trip needled her. So
what if San Francisco had been a catastrophe, net-
ting her no job and no money to help her sister set
up a new life away from Mia's terrible soon-to-be
ex-husband. She was alive and ready to find a steady
job if it killed her, and nothing—especially not her
own paranoia—was going to delay that. Still, she
wished she could rewind the afternoon and make a
different decision, to choose to linger in the shabby
old family home with the cracked tile in the kitchen
and the screen door that didn't quite close. There
were plenty of flaws in that house, but the biggest of
all was that it was simply a house now, not a home.
That was what had driven her out to the beach, the
solace of waves, the healing salt air.

She sucked in a deep breath, pulled her long black
hair back from her face and squared her shoulders.
Common sense returned in a rush.

Why shouldn't she march right out of the water
and climb up to the dock where she'd left her sketch

pad and pastels? The man with the cell phone was just a tourist, gazing out across the waves toward the tiny resort island accessible only by boat, shrouded here and there by clusters of mangroves. It was the place where Antonia did not dare allow her glance to wander. Isla Marsopa. Porpoise Island.

Reuben Sandoval was there, she'd heard, still trying to resurrect the dilapidated resort. She knew Reuben was advertising for a painter, someone to create a beautiful fresco for his hotel, but she would rather walk across a bed of burning coals than become involved with him again. There was only a tiny part of her that did not echo with memories of Reuben, and she was desperate to keep that smallest bit intact.

The man looked up from his phone perusal, eyes flicking across the pristine white sand, then returning to settle on her. What was it about him that struck her as familiar? She bent and made a pretense of examining the ivory perfection of a lady slipper shell. Out of the corner of her eye she saw him dial his phone, eyes glued to her as he did so, and flick a glance toward his watch.

It hit her. His chunky gold watch, worn low and loose on his slender wrist, caught the sunlight. Could it be the same watch worn by the driver who had trailed her for miles from the airport? He'd passed her at times, eyeing her so closely it made her blood run cold, before he fell back to trail her some more.

Her heart thudded. Was he sent by her brother-in-law, hoping she would lead him to where her sister was in hiding after her release from jail? Hector would do anything to get his daughter, Gracie, back, and to punish Mia for taking her. After a long moment, the man tucked the phone in his pocket, straightened his sleeve and walked away toward the end of the dock.

Relief and embarrassment tumbled inside her. *Wrong about the watch, Antonia.* Plenty of guys have gold watches, and she couldn't see it clearly from this distance. She was truly paranoid. After having a drug runner for a brother-in-law and her sister thrown in jail for attempted murder, maybe it wasn't such an unexpected turn of events.

She dug her toes into the sand, drawing comfort from the sensation that there was ground under her feet, even if she couldn't see it through the agitated water. With a sigh that was caught up by the spiraling wind, she headed back toward the dock, stopping suddenly when the man appeared on the beach, his leather shoes out of place, scuffling through the sand.

Her pulse skipped faster as he put himself between her and the dock. She looked for someone else, anyone else, but the beach was quiet except for the slapping of the waves.

Antonia, take control. The solution was easy. No need for panic. She would swim a mile or so down the coast to another perfect cove that was much more popular, storms notwithstanding. She'd come back later for her art supplies. She was wearing a tank top and shorts instead of a swimsuit, but no matter. This man in his leather loafers and blazer was not about to follow her into the ocean. Problem solved.

She sloshed out to deeper water and paddled past the sheltered cove. The pull of the tide was strong, but so was she. Ignoring the spray tossed by the wind that stung her eyes, she kept a steady pace until she was a good fifteen feet in. In the distance the swaying cabbage palms that dotted Isla Marsopa bent under the increasing pressure of the storm. The familiar twinge twisted her gut as she thought about her past with Reuben Sandoval, exploring that tiny paradise.

Keep swimming, she told herself fiercely. Paralleling the shore, she fought the tumbling waves, making her arduous way up the coast, intermittently treading water to preserve her strength. In the distance she caught sight of the dock where Reuben kept his beloved boat and, for a painful moment, she wondered if he had painted over the name on the stern, *Black-Eyed Beauty,* his nickname for her.

Her black-eyed beauty was not enough to help him see the truth about his brother. Even when Hector Sandoval tried to kill her sister and Mia acted in self-defense, Reuben took his brother's side and turned his back on Antonia and Mia, insisting to the police Hector had left the drug trade behind when their father died five years prior. She had to admit Hector had been convincing; both she and her sister believed he was on the straight and narrow, too, for a time. How wrong they'd been. Every one of them. The mistake had cost Mia everything, and Antonia the man she had loved more than anyone else on earth. *Black-Eyed Beauty*—now the name stung like salt in a fresh wound.

She didn't have time to wallow in any more painful memories as she heard an unexpected sound, the throb of a Jet Ski engine. Swimming in little circles, she tried to locate the source, but the waves made it difficult. Over the cresting foam, she caught a glimpse of a Jet Ski moving slowly, the driver twisting his head around as if he were looking for something.

Not something. Her nerves sizzled.

Someone.

Her.

She suddenly realized this person was somehow connected to the gold watch man on the beach. Either that or she was completely crazy.

But the man on the Jet Ski was not out for a relaxing evening jaunt.

Her plan to swim up the coast was in serious jeopardy unless she could outwait him, outlast his game of cat and mouse. Tucking her chin low, she began to tread water, waiting for the cat to lose interest.

* * *

Reuben Sandoval tried again to sew a patch on the canvas awning that protected his boat from the elements. The material frayed, giving way like sand through his fingers until he threw the patch down in disgust. The thing was beyond repair, a feeling he'd begun to have lately about everything in his life.

The Isla Marsopa Hotel was deteriorating faster than he could patch it together. Ironic, since his brother, Hector, had enough money—the riches left behind by their father—to transform Isla into a place that would rival the finest hotels in Florida. But Hector would not touch Isla because it had been their mother's, and Reuben would not ask for the same reason. And others. Their family had fractured neatly down the middle the night their mother snatched the boys from their father, Arlo, to pull them away from the drug trade, only to die less than a year later in a car accident. It had taken Reuben many years to understand her decision to leave, and his brother never had. One thing he knew with absolute clarity: he would not touch one penny of their tainted inheritance.

Reuben meant to restore the three-story Victorian jewel on his own, with whatever money he could earn from his struggling citrus grove. How could he not? Yes, the hotel was ramshackle and the guest bungalows outdated, but the grounds looked out on an ocean panorama that was unparalleled, and the rest of the island was a nature preserve, which ensured its wild beauty would remain unspoiled. Accessible only by boat, the island curved gently, embracing—it seemed to Reuben—the mangrove islands and lagoon in its sandy arms. With its old-world charm, Isla was the perfect getaway, and he knew it was the reason his mother had clung so desperately to this one asset left to her by her father. It was, quite simply, breathtaking.

Something bumped against his leg, and he bent to give the aged tabby a scratch. "Hey, Charley. Didn't go fishing today, so I don't have a treat for you. Weather's not good, buddy."

Charley pushed against Reuben's hand, poking at him with a sandpapery nose. The cat ought to understand about bad weather. His mother found the half-drowned kitten shivering under an overturned boat in the wake of Hurricane Charley that blasted down on the island. Reuben cast an uneasy glance at the sky.

"Going to blow into a hurricane," a gravelly voice said.

Reuben wasn't surprised he hadn't heard Silvio approach. The grizzled old man seemed sometimes to be part of the sand and surf and wind—always there, always had been. Behind him trailed a black man with an affable grin.

"Is that your vote or from the National Hurricane Center?" Reuben said.

"Don't need anyone to tell me. Know it."

Reuben nodded to the younger man. "You think so, too, Gav?"

Gavin scooped up the cat, which purred in delight. "Dunno. I'm from San Diego, remember? This hurricane stuff is your department. I'm just here to collect the meager pittance you provide me. Once I earn my master's, I'm settling permanently in the Golden State. It's safe there."

"Yeah, those earthquakes are a piece of cake," Reuben said.

Gavin waved a hand. "They'll clean up from that last one eventually. It'll cost a chunk of change, though, and speaking of change…"

Reuben laughed. "Yeah, I remember." He fished a crumpled check from his pocket. "It's payday."

"Muchas gracias, Señor Sandoval," Gavin said.

"De nada, Señor Campbell, and your Spanish is horrendous, by the way."

With a smile, Gavin turned to go. Reuben wanted to let him. There was so much to do on the island, and there would be significant damage to repair after the storm receded, his mind added grimly, but he could not risk any lives. "Gav, take the extra boat and get back to the mainland. I'll contact you after the storm passes."

Gavin squinted. "I'm okay. I can hunker down in a bungalow until it's over."

Reuben shook his head. "This isn't a run-of-the-mill storm. I'll send Silvio and Paula with you."

"Ain't going," Silvio said. "Haven't secured all the windows. We've got a day or two yet anyway."

Reuben doubted Paula, Silvio's wife, would be interested in leaving any more than her husband.

Gavin crossed his arms. "What if I say I ain't going either?"

"I'd say I'm your boss and you're fired."

Gavin broke into a wide smile. "When you put it that way… I'll go get my pack. Call you after the storm passes."

Reuben cast an eye along the surf again, surprised to see someone on a Jet Ski plowing through the choppy water.

"I'll take care of the windows," Silvio said.

"There's no way I can crowbar you off this island, is there, old man?" he said, a mixture of love and exasperation blowing through him.

Silvio scratched his chin. "'Course not. You should go. I'm tougher than you, boy."

Reuben laughed. After losing two fingers and sight in his left eye in Korea, Silvio just might be right. "But your wife is tougher than both of us put together, and if she's staying, I guess we all are."

Silvio sighed, the clouds painting odd shadows on his wrinkled face.

They both turned to follow the progress of the Jet Ski, which seemed to be puttering in aimless loops.

"Always one with no sense," Silvio said. "Some tourist gonna get himself drowned for sure and wash up here for me to deal with."

Reuben had to agree. If it was idiotic to stay on the island with an approaching tropical storm that was likely to morph into a hurricane, it was lunacy to be out prancing around on a Jet Ski at such a time.

The guy continued to travel in circles, stopping every so often to peer down into the water.

"Engine trouble maybe?" Reuben hazarded.

Silvio answered with a snort. "More likely doesn't know how to run the thing. Rented it thinking he was going to be some sort of expert." He plucked at a hair in his sparse beard.

Reuben was already moving toward his boat. The little nineteen-foot Bowrider was not much to look at and certainly not enough to enchant resort guests, but it was plenty able to get this nut back to land before he drowned himself.

"Leave him be," Silvio muttered.

Reuben eyed the sun, which was beginning to sink into a clouded horizon. "Only another half hour before sunset."

"Too bad. He can learn to respect the ocean the hard way."

Gruff words from the guy who was following Reuben on board and helping him cast off. As they motored out, Reuben fought the wheel to keep the boat steady against waves determined to drive them off course.

The man seemed oblivious to their approach. He wore no life jacket over his massive, bare shoulders, water lashing his face, which was still too far away to see clearly. Stupid, but sturdy.

Reuben was amazed at how quickly the storm had worsened even in the past half hour. The Jet Ski driver had no doubt been taken by surprise as well, though he continued to meander rather than making for shore. "Hey," Reuben called over the sound of the engine.

The man didn't hear him.

Reuben edged the boat closer, ten feet away, until the guy looked up, face slack with surprise. "We can take you back," Reuben shouted. "Climb aboard and we'll tow the ski."

The man didn't react. Reuben assumed he hadn't heard and was about to repeat the message when the craft abruptly turned around and sped off toward the Florida coast, heaving on the angry waves.

Reuben shot a look at Silvio, who was shaking his head. "Told you. Thickheaded. He's got to learn the hard way."

Reuben's stomach tightened for some reason he could not fathom. He did not think the man had been circling in the midst of a storm for pleasure. There was something intense about the hostile stare, the tight mouth—something cold and hard. Contrary to

Reuben's assessment, the guy was obviously quite competent on his Jet Ski.

Silvio patted his shoulder. "Come on, boy. Enough good deeds. Back now. Got to batten down."

Reuben snapped out of his reverie after one more look at the departing jet skier, who was nearly out of sight. He was ready to push back toward Isla when something caught his eye, a glimmer of color that did not match the angry gray of the sea. He looked again and saw only the roiling surf.

"Let's go," Silvio repeated.

"Hang on," Reuben said, wiping the spray from his face. "I saw something." Seconds ticked into a full minute. Another glimmer—yellow. Something yellow. His heart contracted. A swimmer?

"Hold her steady," he shouted to Silvio as he climbed to the edge of the boat and over the metal railing, which was heaving so violently he could not hope to fish the woman, or whatever it was, out of the water.

"Ya crazy, boy?"

Reuben ignored him as he pinpointed the location of the yellow flash and dove in. The violence of the water disoriented him, and he closed his mouth to keep from swallowing. Now he could see nothing but a wall of ocean, pitching and heaving around him. He did a slow circle, salt stinging his eyes.

Silvio's right. You are crazy. It had probably been a plastic bag or a towel lost by a careless beachgoer, certainly not a woman. He turned to swim back to the boat when he saw it again, only this time he was not imagining it.

Out of the gray surge he saw a woman's raised hand, silhouetted for a moment against the waning sun. Then the waves rose up between them and she disappeared.

TWO

Antonia realized the error in her plan. Though the water was in the seventy-degree range, her teeth had begun to chatter and the inactivity left her chilled and numb. She couldn't see the man on the water-craft at the moment, but she knew he could stay on that Jet Ski much longer than she could tread water. It was too far to shore, and even Isla Marsopa was impossible for her to reach without being seen.

Panic began to edge up in her gut as the waves slapped harder at her face and shoulders. She was beginning to lose her sense of direction as the cold gripped her. At one point she thought she heard a motor, but the roaring sea confused her ears. The sky was dimming. Soon it would be too dark for him to spot her, but it would also be impossible for her to find her way back to shore.

She would be adrift, gradually sucked under into a dark void until her lungs filled with water.

Antonia knew there were many more lives hanging in the balance than her own. If she died, who would help support Mia and Gracie? Who would send the small payments to their mother, who had moved into a trailer home in Jacksonville when she could no longer manage the house? Antonia tried to quell the panic and kicked harder to keep her chin above water. Soon she would have no choice but to make for Isla Marsopa and hope she could avoid detection. She did not allow herself to imagine what Reuben would say if she managed to make it to his shore.

What seemed like an endless amount of time went by before she realized she could not even hear the Jet Ski anymore, nor could she spot the driver's bulky form over the cresting waves. Had he really gone? A wall of water obscured everything else from view. She did not dare believe it, but gone or not, she had to make for Isla before she drowned. She remembered her father's voice, patient and soft, teaching her to swim when she was a child. *Let the water hold you up, Antonia. Don't fight it.*

She tried to relax, but her fear had risen high enough to override good sense. Forcing her arms into action, she pushed in what she hoped was the right direction. Waves sucked and pulled at her and every stroke was a fight. Chin down, she fought as hard as she could against the ocean, but, like her father also reminded her many times before he passed, *The ocean always wins.*

She would not let it win now. Teeth gritted, she kicked hard and cut through the waves, making what she thought was good progress until she stopped to rest and felt herself being sucked back toward the mainland, in spite of her efforts to tread water.

Father God, help me.

It was dark now, and a spatter of rain had begun to fall. Her ears rang with the sound of the ocean. Ahead she imagined she saw a light. Had she gone farther than she thought? Was it the light from the old hotel? A boat? With a final burst of energy she fought her way toward it until her arm came into contact unexpectedly with something soft and pliable. She grabbed at it, but her fingers slipped loose.

Then a hand took hold of her wrist, and she felt herself being towed along. Poor light and the spray of surf and rain made it impossible to see who was dragging her along, but she knew it did not matter anyway. Staying in the ocean meant death. She tried to kick her feet and help her rescuer, but her legs had become so cold and numb she was a helpless weight.

Then there was a boat. Cold metal. Calloused hands reaching down. Strong arms holding her up. Wind teasing goose bumps onto her skin. A familiar old man plucked her from the ocean, leading her to a seat and wrapping a musty blanket that smelled faintly of trout around her shoulders.

She was shaking so badly that her vision blurred. Blinking hard and clamping her jaw shut to keep her teeth from rattling, she shook the hair from her face and looked into the broad cheekbones, the full lips, the chin with a scar and those eyes that held so many secrets. Reuben Sandoval stood on the heaving deck, water dripping from his cropped hair, molding the T-shirt and shorts around his lithe body.

She was too cold to feel surprise, shock, dismay or any other emotion. It was as if she had landed in a strange dream and the only functioning part of her body was the part that said, *Thank You, God, that I am alive.*

Reuben knelt on the deck and looked intently at her, as if he were trying to convince himself what he saw was real. He said something in a voice so low she could not hear it over her chattering teeth. He reached toward her, and for a brief moment she felt a combined terror and longing. Instead of embracing her, he pulled the blanket more firmly around her shoulders.

Then he took the captain's chair next to her and asked Silvio, the old man whom she recognized, to take them back.

Back where?

To the mainland where her small battered house waited?

To the dock where she remembered suddenly she'd left her art supplies?

To Isla Marsopa, she realized through her confusion.

To the island where her heart had been torn apart by a storm fiercer than any hurricane.

* * *

Reuben should have felt deep shock at finding it was Antonia Verde he'd just fished out of the Atlantic Ocean, but for some reason, he felt more confusion than anything else. Antonia was never far from his thoughts or his memories in the year they'd been apart. Reminders of her lingered in the warm sand where they'd hunted for shells. They survived in the crisp air that made her hair dance across her laughing face and the Florida sun that bronzed her perfect skin. He'd known she'd returned; he'd heard as much from his brother.

Hector kept it simple. *The little traitor is back, Reuben. Look out.*

Mia had energetically sought to destroy his brother and excuse her own mistakes by accusing Hector of attacking her, forcing her to defend herself. Upon Mia's release from jail, she'd taken Gracie and run, leaving his brother desperately missing his little girl. Reuben suspected that Antonia knew perfectly well where her sister was holing up and was probably even helping her. Still, the sight of her shivering, clutching the blanket around herself as if it were some sort of armor, twisted his stomach. The traitor, the lush-lipped, silk-skinned traitor who killed him on the inside, still charged his body with a rush of feeling.

"I need to go back to the mainland," she said, after a few stuttering attempts to speak.

"Too dark," Reuben said.

She looked as though she wanted to respond, but the shivering turned into full-on trembling and she hunched deeper into the blanket.

Fine by him. Silence was probably the better of many options that would lead to angry words. Again. Curiosity burned inside him and he longed to question her, but instead he helped Silvio tie up to the dock after they fought the waves back to Isla Marsopa. Silvio helped Antonia out, and Reuben followed them into the main house, where a light shone in the lower level.

Paula met them in the lobby. Her red hair had long ago faded, overcome by gray, but her eyes sparked in her tan face. "Antonia Verde?" She blinked with recognition. "What happened out there?"

"Let's get her something warm to drink," Reuben said, temporarily staunching the explanation that he, too, was eager to hear.

Reuben gestured toward a wooden chair and fetched another blanket as Paula heated some water for tea. He was relieved that they hadn't lost power yet. The generator had been fussy and he hadn't had time to tinker with it.

Paula wrapped a nubby wool blanket around Reuben's shoulders and handed them each a cup of hot tea. Antonia clutched hers with both hands, delicate fingers cupping the mug and holding it close to her chest.

"Gotten yourself into more trouble, I see," Paula said. "And dragged Reuben along."

Antonia looked up, and a tiny flash of spirit returned to her features. Reuben felt a swell of relief and something else deep in his core.

"I didn't ask for anyone's help," Antonia said.

Paula sniffed. "Reuben isn't the kind to let a person drown, even if that person is an enemy."

Antonia stiffened. "I'm sorry to cause trouble."

Gavin came in, a pack on his shoulder. "I was ready to head back to the mainland, but I couldn't find you…." He broke off when he saw Antonia. "Who are you?"

"Antonia Verde," she said through chattering teeth.

Gavin's eyebrows shot up. "Here I thought you were trying to get people off this island, Mr. Sandoval."

Reuben would have laughed in different circumstances. "Storm's worse. You'll have to bunk here for the night, Gav. I'll take you back at first light."

Gavin shrugged. "Sure thing. One more of Paula's meals will make it worthwhile."

Paula's face broke into a rare smile. "You're a flatterer, Mr. Campbell."

"My grammy says flattery will get you nowhere, but I find it usually scores me a second piece of pie."

Reuben worked out a plan. "Paula, can you get the Seabreeze ready? It's the only bungalow that's relatively decent."

"If that's what you want," Paula said. "Mr. Campbell, set the table for dinner, please."

Gavin sighed. "If I could only convince her to call me Gav." He set about plopping silverware haphazardly on the oval dining table.

Paula gave Antonia a final glare and went out, Silvio following.

"Thanks, but there's just no way I can spend the night here," Antonia said.

"Unless you're going to swim back, I don't see much of a choice for you." Reuben kept his tone level. "What happened?"

She avoided looking at him. "I swam out too far."

"I got that. Who was on the Jet Ski, and what did he want with you?"

She sipped tea without seeming to taste it. "I don't know. I think he might have been sent by a guy who followed me from the airport earlier. He was watching me from the beach, so I thought I'd swim up the coast and avoid them both."

Two guys? He felt a tightening in his gut. "Why are they after you?"

Antonia put the mug down on the antique trunk that served as a coffee table, her hands trembling. "Like I said, I don't know. It could be just my imagination."

It was unlike her to be guarded. "Better call the cops."

Antonia shook her head, sending droplets of water

through the lamp-lit lobby. "It's nothing. Probably a misunderstanding."

"Don't think so. Cops are a good idea."

Her eyes flashed at him. "The cops already believe I lied to support my sister, and so do you." The words wobbled a bit at the end, and he saw her swallow hard.

He took the brunt of it, the anger that flowed from her and was nearly a match for his own. He spoke lower, hoping Gavin wasn't hearing every word. "Keep the past out of this."

"I'd be happy to." Antonia stood, discarding the blanket, chafing her arms to warm up. He remembered the softness of those arms, tender, loving, and the memory awakened an ache deep inside. He stood, too, walking to the window and looking out toward the restless sea. He drew close to her, close enough to imagine he could feel the warmth of her skin, hear the soft purr of her breathing. Close, but far enough away to remember what she'd done.

"Stay the night. I'll take you back in the morning if the storm will allow."

Antonia was staring at the spotted junonia shell nestled on the marble fireplace hearth. "It's the same one, isn't it?" she said, voice low.

He didn't answer.

She traced a finger over the broken edge, and he was drowned in the memory. Happy times, her finding the lovely specimen, him ready to throw the broken shell back into the surf.

"No, keep it," she'd insisted. "It's been damaged, but that makes it more beautiful." She'd kissed him and run off to find another shell, leaving the broken junonia in his fingers.

He'd loved her for that, for finding beauty in the brokenness. He watched now as she carefully replaced the shell on the mantel and turned to face him with none of the tenderness he had yearned for in those black, beautiful eyes.

"I'll walk you to the bungalow," he said.

Gavin made no comment as he watched them go.

Antonia could not see much as they made their way over the dark path, wind chilling her even further. She was relieved to find that Paula and Silvio had gone, leaving a lamp on to illuminate the wood flooring and stonework above a tiny fireplace. A little settee with cheerful blue-striped cushions complemented the azure bookcase. It must be Paula's work as Reuben was color-blind, which was why he usually wore all black to make the matching easier. Or maybe the decor was another woman's contribution. Not hard to believe; Reuben was a poet at heart, gorgeous, loyal, and in the past one look from his chocolate eyes made her weak in the knees.

She swallowed the thought.

Reuben cleared his throat and shoved his hands

into his pockets, a gesture she knew he'd learned in his childhood.

"Paula left you a change of clothes."

Antonia saw the faded Gators sweatshirt and pants. The housekeeper hadn't handed them over cheerfully, she was sure, but Antonia was in no position to be fussy. She could not wait to exchange her soaking garments for dry ones.

Reuben opened a small cupboard and handed her a flashlight. "Storm may take out our electricity, but we've reinforced the walls so it's more up to code than the main house."

He turned to go.

"Thank you," she blurted. "I mean, thank you for getting me out of the water and, um, letting me stay here—just until morning."

He smiled—a shy grin, like a teen after his first kiss. She could not look away from his lips, expressive and sculpted perfectly. Tender, she remembered, and loaded with promises. Promises he could not keep.

"You'll be our last guest of the season." Something sad flickered across his face.

"You haven't made much progress on the hotel?"

"Dry July and August and frost last December messed up the oranges. Not a lot of cash to funnel into this place. I managed to fix up two rooms in the main house and this bungalow, so we've had only a few paying customers."

His gaze ran over the wooden beams.

The irony confused her. Hector was rolling in money, yet Reuben struggled. *But when push came to shove,* she reminded herself, *he had his brother's back, not yours.*

"I'll be ready first thing in the morning," she said, trying for a stronger tone than a dripping wet, exhausted woman should command.

"We'll get you there as soon as we can. By morning we should have a better forecast on the storm." He hesitated. "Nee…"

The endearment cut at her, and she saw that he regretted the slip.

Memories flitted through her mind.

"Why are you staring at me?"

His smile, those lips. "The light in your eyes, it's like the sky just before the sun rises."

She looked feverishly around the room. "Nice. Nice place."

"Antonia, your life isn't my business anymore, but if you were scared enough of that man on the Jet Ski to risk drowning, you should talk to the cops. I can arrange…"

"No," she said quickly. "I don't want you to arrange anything. I'm sorry I wound up here, Reuben. Believe me, it wasn't my intention. I appreciate your help, but I'll go tomorrow."

"And then disappear again."

"That's what you want, isn't it?" She swallowed. "The best thing for both of us."

His gaze hardened, and she knew what was coming. "Where's Gracie?"

"I don't know."

"Yes, you do. You're helping your sister break the law. Ironic, since that's what you accused my brother of doing."

"She asked me to help her do what she had to do because Gracie's life is more important than your brother's selfishness."

"It's not selfish to want to see your child. He loves Gracie."

"He put her in danger by getting back into the business. He attacked her mother."

"He didn't…" Reuben broke off, the muscles around his jaw working. "There's no point getting into it now." He exhaled. "You will probably never believe this, but he misses Gracie, and so do I. More than I can say."

Without another word he opened the door and walked into the night.

She watched him from the window, standing behind the curtain in case he might turn around again and catch her there. He stopped at the bend in the path, looking not back at the bungalow, but straight ahead at the delicate peaked roof of the main house, wondering perhaps how it would escape the storm without damage. It struck her that she'd never considered how Reuben might have felt about losing Gracie. She should have known. In happier times she'd seen him spend hours on the floor stacking blocks or clomping around on his hands and knees pretending to be Gracie's trusty palomino. Her throat tightened and tears pricked her eyes.

But Mia was right. Hector was dangerous, and she could not allow him back into her life. And that meant Reuben, too.

All around, the island twisted and bent under the increasing threat. It seemed to her that nothing on Isla Marsopa escaped unscathed. His mother died on her way to the island. Reuben was chained to a disastrously expensive repair. And Antonia herself would never be able to picture Isla without remembering what she had most treasured…and lost.

Her vision blurred and she blinked hard as the darkness swallowed Reuben up. Tomorrow she would choose to face the wrath of the storm, no matter how strong, rather than revisit the tattered wreck of her past with Reuben. It would be kinder for both of them.

THREE

Reuben was prowling the hotel grounds long before sunup, and the massive cloud wall illuminated by the moon didn't bode well for the coming day. The scenario was all too grimly familiar. He and everyone else from Jamaica to the eastern seaboard had been tracking the progress of the monstrous storm, which started as a tropical wave that ballooned over the west coast of Africa before strengthening into a depression. From there it burgeoned into a tropical storm that parked for a while over the Caribbean Sea, taunting almost, before launching itself into what the National Hurricane Center had officially deemed a bona fide hurricane. It would strike land in less than forty-eight hours.

He swallowed a sick feeling. Hurricane Charley had been a Category 4 with wind speeds of 130 miles per hour. The hotel had barely survived. This approaching menace, which had now been named Hurricane Tony, was projected to equal or surpass that rating.

He arrived in the kitchen and grabbed a piece of the succulent green banana and pork patties left over from Paula's delectable meal the night before. She'd been cooking all his favorites lately. The worse things got, the more Paula cooked. As he savored each bite, he decided to make a renewed effort to get her and Silvio off the island. And, of course, Antonia. His thoughts wandered to the tiny bungalow.

He wondered if she had been warm enough. Perhaps he should have lit a fire or brought her a snack…. He mentally chided himself. *Over and done. She's not yours to worry about.* As he wrestled the front door open to round up boards and nails, he stopped short. A boat was moored next to his. An expensive cabin cruiser that looked out of place against the rickety dock. He froze, thinking whoever had been after Antonia the night before had come to finish the job.

He'd sprinted a yard down the path toward the bungalow when a voice stopped him.

"Slow down before you hurt yourself."

His brother stood at the side entrance to the hotel, a cigarette held between his slender fingers. He flashed a lazy smile. "We need to talk, brother."

Reuben sighed in relief and joined Hector on the veranda, where he got a better look at the bruise darkening his cheekbone. "What happened?"

Hector shrugged and shot a look at the roiling sea. "Inside. No need to stand in the rain."

"Lose the cigarette," Reuben said.

Hector did so without the usual flippant comment.

Reuben followed his younger brother inside, suddenly colder than he had been moments before. The hotel lobby was gloomy, quiet, as though the old building itself was waiting for the storm to land.

Hector paced in front of the bay window, and Reuben let him do so without interruption. You couldn't hurry Hector, no matter how hard you tried.

When he'd gazed out at the wind-lashed palms for a while, and then seemingly studied every inch of the pine molding and floors, he turned around. "There's trouble coming. I tried to keep it from you, but it's bigger than me."

Reuben braced himself. That his brother would admit to weakness was the most telling thing. He was not talking about the storm. "Who?"

Hector broke off, eyes narrowing as the floorboards creaked. "Who's that?"

Gavin came into the room, his expression sheepish. "Sorry. Didn't want to interrupt." He held up his pack. "Thought the boat was leaving."

Reuben introduced Gavin to his brother.

"A pleasure," Hector said in a voice that indicated it was anything but.

"I'll just go back upstairs. Call me when you're ready to go." He left.

Hector waited a long moment before he resumed. "It's Garza. He wants Isla."

Reuben steeled himself. "He's always wanted it." It was the perfect hub for him to get his drugs into Florida. The Garza family, led by Frank Garza, was in tight with the Colombian drug lords who flew their products to the Bahamas, using a number of ingenious methods to get it to prearranged spots in the ocean where speedboats would pick it up. What Garza needed was a piece of land with few people to interfere, within close proximity to the mainland, from which he could set loose his fleet of speedboats for any given operation, so many that the coast guard could not possibly nab the one vessel that held the illicit cargo.

"He's decided it's time to acquire it. Now."

Reuben groaned inwardly. Plenty of dark shallow shoals around Isla where boats could lead authorities on a goose chase if it came down to it. Isla was perfect. Garza had sent people before with offers to buy. When he'd declined, one of Reuben's bungalows had mysteriously burned down and his best boat had been scuttled. "I told him to his face that Isla was mine and I won't sell it at any price, and he's not going to bully me into handing it over."

"And he believed you," Hector said with a wry smile. "That is why he means to take it without your permission."

Reuben studied his brother. "So he's asked you to persuade me?"

"I refused, of course. My guy, Benny, arrived before they got too far into trying to convince me, but he knows we are close and so he asked me to tell you as a courtesy. I guess he thinks since we were in the same business together once, I will understand the urgency of his request. I do. He's dead serious, Reuben."

"I can't believe this. I'll go to the cops."

"If you wish, but you and I both know that's a waste of effort. You can never get any proof to stick on Garza. He's like Teflon."

Reuben's mind raced. He forced himself to say it. "Hector, you're clean, right? You weren't trying to leverage your way back into the business using Isla?" He waited for his brother to face him, to look deep into his eyes and proclaim he had not returned to running the cocaine trade that had made his father rich.

Hector's eyes burned, and Reuben knew he'd made a mistake. "It was not enough to have my wife almost kill me because she didn't believe me? I'm to repeat it over and over to you, brother?" Hector closed the gap between them. "I made a promise to you. I was out of it. I promised Mia, too, but she wouldn't believe me, and now I have no wife and she took my child." His voice cracked slightly. "My wife, my daughter. Don't tell me it will cost me my brother, too."

Reuben gripped his brother's shoulder. "No, it won't."

Hector allowed a tight smile, his gaze wandering around the aged kitchen. He touched the bruise on his cheek. "Isla is a wreck, you know. Maybe it's not worth it."

Anger flamed inside Reuben's gut. It was worth everything. The old hotel and the island on which it barely stood were their mother's legacy, the shining piece of hope she held on to when her husband took up drug running, when he turned into someone she could no longer respect. "I won't let it go."

"Our mother wouldn't, either," Hector spat, "and now she's dead."

The past crackled between them like lightning. "We've been through this. She wanted more for us."

He shook his head. "She ran."

"She felt she had no choice."

"Our father loved her, worshipped her, like I did Mia."

"Our father worked for drug runners."

"Yet she did not mind the nice clothes, the private schools for her boys, the trips. She didn't protest about those things, did she?"

"She stopped respecting him, Hector, and that was the end." He added quietly, "You can't force someone to love you." That lesson was ground into him, at least.

Hector did not answer.

A palm branch slapped against the window. Reuben took a deep breath and stepped back. It was not the time. "I'm not giving Isla to anyone."

Hector sighed. "I know, and I would be disappointed if you gave in. I just needed to warn you. There's more coming at you than a hurricane, and you were never the ruthless type."

Ruthless, Reuben thought, is a relative term. Though he wanted nothing more than to live a quiet life with his orange groves and to shuttle guests to and from the island, it might be necessary to fight.

I'm not afraid of a fight, little brother.

Not afraid at all.

Antonia hurried through the rain to the main house, hoping there might be some instant coffee she could help herself to before anyone else awoke. Truth was, she was hungry, too, but she would not take food from Reuben. It seemed wrong to take anything from him now.

Letting herself in quietly, she saw Reuben standing, hands on hips, face a mask of irritation or concern, she could not tell. She stopped in the doorway, uncertain. She'd just made up her mind to turn around and go see if she could find Silvio and convince him to ferry her without involving Reuben when, to her horror, Hector stepped out of the shadows, seeming not the least bit surprised to see her.

"Like the cat that keeps coming back," Hector said, giving her the once-over.

Antonia straightened, wishing she didn't look quite so much like a half-drowned tabby. "I didn't come back. I had an accident. Reuben is giving me a lift back to the mainland."

"He isn't hard enough to hold a grudge," Hector said, eyes narrowing. "But I am."

Reuben moved between them. "Not now."

Hector shrugged. "We are finished with our talk. Don't stay here, Reuben. It's dangerous."

Antonia noted the look between the two Sandovals.

"I'm going up to the cupola. I want to see this monster storm approaching. Maybe I will stay here and ride it out." Hector walked close to her to pass by. She felt her nerves go taut, and she cemented her feet to the floor.

"You know that I will find my daughter," he murmured.

"No," she shot back. "You won't touch her."

He smiled. "Oh, yes. I will spend every penny and every remaining minute of my life until I find Mia, and then she will return to jail for stealing my daughter from me."

Antonia felt her fingers balling into fists. "You won't get a chance to hurt them again."

"When Mia tried to kill me, she ended her right to be Gracie's mother."

"She figured out you were dealing drugs. You attacked her and she defended herself. She paid for that decision by going to jail, but now she's free and you have no hold on her anymore."

"You and your sister, you are trash, from a family of peasants." Spittle gleamed on his lips.

It felt as if she had been slapped. Her father had been a fisherman, her mother a seamstress. Hard-working people who toiled every day of their lives to provide for their girls. And Hector, the man who never had an honest job, would dare to speak of them with such disdain?

Through the anger that nearly blinded her, she realized Reuben had stepped between them. He was inches from Hector. "Don't talk to her like that."

Hector's eyes flashed. "She's…"

"I don't care," Reuben said in a quiet voice that had the current of danger running through it. "You will not speak to her that way," he repeated.

Antonia felt the tension ribboning through Reuben's back, through the set of his muscles, the squaring of his jaw. She felt a flash of gratefulness.

Hector offered a half smile. "I was right. In spite of everything, you still have feelings for her."

Reuben flushed. "I will not tolerate you disrespecting her, or any other woman, in my presence. We weren't raised that way."

Hector looked once more at Antonia and then stepped back. "I'm going up now." He left.

Reuben sighed. "I'm sorry about that."

She was breathing hard, trying not to cry. Gracie,

sweet two-year-old Gracie. How could Mia keep her safe with Hector determined to find them?

Reuben's brown eyes were soft, and he put a hand on her forearm. She pulled away.

"Don't. We both know you think he's right."

"No." Reuben shook his head. "He's not right, and even if he was, he doesn't get to speak to you like that."

She gulped as he stroked a hand over her hair with the lightest touch. "No one will disrespect you around me." His fingers trailed down her hair, onto her shoulder and dropped away, leaving a trickle of sparks behind. "Ever."

She breathed hard, trying to gain some control over her stampeding emotions. Quickly she gripped his hand and then released it.

He turned away. "We'll get you out of here as soon as it's full light."

Skin still tingling, she grabbed hold of the threads of common sense. Hector was bad, and supporting him made Reuben bad, too. She found that she had twirled a strand of her black hair tightly around her index finger. Quickly she let it go. "I'll wait in the bungalow."

"You don't have to. Stay here."

She wanted to stay, to sit in the worn cushioned chairs in this place that had once been a charming respite, to put away the horrible memories and re-member the precious ones, like the chipped junonia shell that now caught the feeble light of dawn. Instead she turned a bit unsteadily and headed into the storm-charged morning.

Reuben went through the motions mechanically; downing a glass of orange juice, trying unsuccessfully again to persuade Silvio and Paula to leave the island, compiling a mental list of things to purchase on the mainland when he dropped off Antonia. Nails, more water, extra batteries, and then back to the island to secure the boats as best he could. None of the preparations dispelled the discomfort he felt at his brother's visit. Trouble was coming from all fronts. He could not protect his brother; Hector would find a way to take care of himself. But he could, at least, deliver Antonia out of the battle zone. She would never understand why he supported Hector. It cut him. She, like everyone else, would forever believe the Sandoval boys guilty of their father's sins.

He knew Hector, knew his faults and weaknesses, but he also knew how his brother defended him when they were teens, stood up for him against a crowd of people who believed him guilty of taking advantage of a local girl. The hatred of the community who was all too willing to accept that he'd done it. The sideways looks and sneered remarks of peers who believed the girl's story. Cops with an eagerness to convict him glittering in their eyes right up to the moment when they decided they had no evidence to hold him. All because his last name was Sandoval. And when the half dozen boys cornered him at his uncle's orchard and began to beat him, it was his brother who stood there beside him, taking the punishment, knee-deep in the melee until the cops arrived and broke things up.

That was the real Hector. Wasn't it?

"Enough," Silvio said.

Reuben jerked from his thoughts to find Silvio pointing at the water jug he was filling to overflowing in the sink. He turned off the tap. "I'm taking her back now."

"Good," Paula said.

Silvio chided his wife. "She doesn't deserve that."

Paula didn't answer as she brushed a kiss on Reuben's cheek. "Hurry back. Don't want you caught in the storm."

"Yes, ma'am," Reuben said. He gestured to Silvio to follow him outside and told him about Garza's threat. "You should take Paula away."

"I'll tell her, but she won't budge."

Reuben experienced twin pangs of both tenderness and worry. The emotions quickened his pace as he hurried to the *Black-Eyed Beauty,* his breathing edging up a notch when he saw Antonia waiting there, black hair ribboning around her like wings.

Gavin joined them and stood uncharacteristically

quietly on the dock a few paces behind. He'd have to be blind and deaf not to pick up on the tension between the two of them. He merely whistled to himself and looked at the birds wheeling above the water.

Hector's boat was gone, and Reuben felt a surge of relief. His brother was a distraction he could not afford. He marveled at the thick wall of black clouds, massed like soldiers on the horizon. This hurricane would not retreat until Florida had experienced the full weight of its power. There were no leisure craft to be seen out in the open. The water empty of the usual ocean lovers. Normally he relished the early morning quiet, but now it bothered him. He thought about calling Silvio to make sure he'd locked up, but was annoyed to discover he'd left his cell phone at the hotel.

"Look there," Gavin said, jerking his chin toward the expanse of sea between Isla and the mainland. Just past a clump of black mangroves, a sixteen-foot skimmer tossed up and down on the waves. His gut tightened. Garza had an arsenal of men and boats. Had he decided to start his campaign of intimidation already?

"Whose boat is that?" Gavin asked.

"Not sure." Reuben sent up a prayer that he would be able to deliver Antonia out of the nasty business. She'd been entangled in his family long enough.

Their love was irreparably ruined, but he did not want to see her hurt. He would not allow it.

He blew out a breath when he realized the boat was anchored against the heaving waves. Ridiculous to be out in such weather, but the captain was certainly not one of Garza's men poised to pursue Reuben. Not yet, anyway.

Reuben sucked in a deep breath full of humid air. Exhaling slowly, he tried to summon up a sense of calm as he strode toward the *Black-Eyed Beauty*. The smell hit him, pungent and foul. Gasoline. Moving closer he could make out the puddles on the bottom of the boat, filming the seats, dampening the wooden boards under his feet.

"Gas?" Antonia said, around his shoulder.

The crack of a gun cut through her words. He had time to look up and see the incoming flare as it arced gracefully across the sky, splaying a shower of sparks in its wake. Time stood still, freezing him with terror for one endless second before adrenaline propelled him into action. He turned and shoved Gavin off the dock and into the water.

"Swim, both of you," he yelled, grabbing Antonia's hand and yanking her to the edge of the dock.

She opened her mouth to scream or shout a question, but there was no time. He pushed her off the dock, her slender body neatly cleaving the water.

When she surfaced, he yelled, "Swim away from—"

The boat exploded behind them as the flare ignited the gasoline, fiery splinters spiraling around, painting golden arcs in the chaotic wind.

FOUR

Antonia felt bits of wood raining down, knifing into the water around her. She could not understand at first what had happened. Hot embers landed on her shoulder, burning through the wet fabric of her shirt. An eerie, orange glow lit Reuben's face, and she could see lines of grief there, illuminated for a moment by the remnants of the *Black-Eyed Beauty* that crackled behind her. The sadness there took her by surprise, the naked sorrow now turning to something else before her eyes, something harder, something dangerous.

She swiveled in the water to get a look at the burning boat, which glowed like a torch floating on the restless sea. Another flare sailed through the sky and ignited the other boat docked there, a smaller motorboat that caught fire with a whoosh.

Acrid black smoke blossomed around them. Reuben grabbed her wrist and tugged her away, his grip so strong it hurt. He hauled her until they were out of range of the falling debris.

"What happened?"

Reuben's expression was impossible to read in the weak light, but the intensity of his command was not. "No time now. Swim hard. That way."

Gavin spat out a mouthful of water. "He's right. Do it."

She struck out in the direction he'd pointed, away from the dock and back toward Isla, headed for the gap in the mangrove fringe that proved the most direct route. Waves crested over her head leaving her breathless. The lightening sky proved a small measure of help, silhouetting the island against a backdrop of steel gray clouds, obscured here and there by the heavy foliage.

Part of her mind wanted to mull over the loss Reuben had just experienced. She'd been on or around boats all her life. Her father, a fisherman by trade, was on the ocean nearly every day until his death, and she'd been toted along with him from the time she was a toddler. She knew boats like she knew the vibrant colors of an ocean sunrise or the sound of the beach at night when there was no one around but the scuttling crabs. They were more than wood and engines. They were beloved by their owners, cherished, nurtured…and mourned.

Just swim.

It took all her strength to fight through the water, and even with every ounce of determination she found herself slowing against the storm-strengthened surf.

"Hold on to me. I'll tow us."

She turned off the arguments materializing in her brain and clung to the waistband of Reuben's pants as he charged through the surf. Against her fingers, she felt the muscles of his back working, strong from hours of hard labor in his orange fields and hotel restoration. He'd always been strong. She'd never beat him at arm wrestling, not once besting him on their sprints around the island. She paddled as best she could to help propel them forward.

When she could feel the water shallowing out around them, she let go and began forging her own way toward the beach. Wind plastered her hair to her face and left her shivering as they slogged out of the surf; Gavin reaching out to help her. She longed to throw herself down on the sand, just for a moment, to allow her lungs to catch up, but Reuben grabbed her cold hand.

"Come on."

He was nearly sprinting, and she marveled that he still had so much stamina after their frantic swim. Something was fueling him with an unnatural energy. Fear? Sorrow? Anger. The realization scared her. She scrambled after him, past the packed sand and through the ripple of ornamental grasses and clustered palms thrashing in the wind. Charging under the stately oaks dripping with Spanish moss and finally across the green lawn, they made it to the graveled path to the hotel veranda. Slamming through the front door, Reuben locked it behind them.

Silvio stood there with a phone in his hand, mouth gaping and eyes agog.

His wife ran into the room holding a pair of binoculars. "What happened? We heard an explosion. Silvio was trying to call you."

"Someone blew up my boats," Reuben snarled.

Antonia had seen Reuben angry before only a few times. Anger was not an emotion to which he succumbed to often, but now rage flickered in his eyes like a wakening giant. Snatching the phone from Silvio, he stabbed in the numbers. "I'm calling the cops. The guy doused the dock in gasoline and fired a flare from out there on a skimmer."

Paula's face went slack with horror. "What?"

"Who would do that?" Antonia finally managed around her chattering teeth. His eyes locked on hers, but he did not answer.

"I'd sure like to know the answer to that," Gavin said.

A sinking feeling flooded Antonia's stomach. Hector's mob connections. Crime swirled around his family like a dark, fetid wind. Reuben must have read her thoughts because his mouth twisted.

The cold took over her body, leaving her shivering in the Isla Hotel lobby for the second time in as many days, the lazily turning ceiling fans cooling her even more.

Gavin absently picked up Charley and cradled the cat to his chest while staring at Reuben. "This kind of thing happen to you often, Mr. Sandoval? Pretty dramatic for a guy who grows oranges and runs a hotel on the side."

Something glittered in Gavin's eyes, a calculating look that surprised Antonia. Then again, the kid had a right to be suspicious after nearly being blown up right along with them.

Reuben paced as he waited, muscles in his clenched jaw rippling. "This is Reuben Sandoval. I need to talk to an officer about an attempted murder. Someone just blew up my boats. No, no one is injured. I am positive it was not an accident." He paused. "Myself, an employee and…a guest I was ferrying to the mainland."

Antonia didn't know why the word hurt. They were not anything more than that, two people thrown together by chance. She was a guest on his island, an unwanted one.

Gavin set the cat down and Charley made his way to Antonia, sniffing at the water puddling around her shoes. She reached down to pet him, but the animal avoided her damp fingertips. Instead he sat a safe distance away tucked next to a conch shell on the bottom shelf of a massive bookcase, regarding her with an appraising look. *I don't know what's going on, either,* she wanted to say. *Ask your owner.*

Reuben made three dripping orbits around the lobby with Paula following, trying to thrust a towel around his shoulders. "Yes," he snapped into the phone. "I understand that, but this is urgent. I know there's a hurricane about to make landfall." He blew out a breath. "All right."

He pocketed the phone. "They're prepping for the storm. They can't send an officer out now, but someone will attempt to get here as soon as possible."

"That right?" Silvio lifted a bushy eyebrow. "They don't believe you, do they?"

"No. Cops are not going to believe anything from a Sandoval." He kicked at a box sitting on the floor, punching a hole in the cardboard and making Paula jump. "They destroyed my boats."

Antonia heard something in his tone that made her think he knew exactly who had done it. Paula interrupted her thoughts by going to the closet and getting down a basket of clothes. "Leftovers from the absentminded guests. Go change. Again."

Gavin had already gone upstairs to do the same.

This time she didn't bother to protest, squelching meekly into the tiny bathroom connected to the lobby. Avoiding her reflection in the mirror, which was no doubt ghastly, she changed into the faded jeans that were a size too big and the short-sleeved polo shirt in a pastel-pink color that she would never wear under other circumstances. Paula had even managed a man's navy windbreaker, which extended past her thighs. There was nothing to be done about her sandals except to put them on again. Feeling marginally better, she returned to the lobby.

She found Paula in the kitchen, putting a kettle on to boil. Reuben and Silvio stood on the wide veranda, even more spacious since Reuben had removed all the quaint rockers, binoculars raised to their eyes.

"Do you see the skimmer?" she said, staying well back near the white-painted house to avoid the driving rain.

Reuben did not look at her. "No."

Silvio spoke quietly. "Could be he's headed back to the mainland."

"Or could be he's staying out of open water, hiding out in the lagoon."

"Dangerous," Silvio said. "With the storm coming."

"He's got a reason to finish the job," Reuben said.

Antonia came closer. "What reason?"

A quiet voice interrupted. Hector strolled into the room, his face drawn. "His boss told him to convince you. He will carry out his orders, destroying everything until you capitulate."

Convince Reuben? She took a step backward, a reflexive action.

Reuben appeared just as surprised. "I thought you left."

"I sent Benny back. I wished to stay, to give you a hand with the hurricane preparations." He flashed a distracted smile. "Now I see that you need another kind of help." His smile vanished. "I did not imagine they would act so quickly, so blatantly, believe me. I would have dragged you off this island if I thought…"

Reuben and Hector locked eyes and Antonia could see that Reuben was struggling with some internal decision.

She felt lost. Someone blew up Reuben's boat because their boss ordered them to. She wanted to press, but Reuben turned his back to her and spoke to Silvio. "We have to get her off this island, and Paula, too."

"That's not going to happen now, and you know it as well as I do." Silvio jutted his chin at the ocean. "Both your boats just went up in flames."

"The police…"

Hector laughed. "The hurricane makes landfall within hours. Police aren't coming." His tone was bitter. "Not for a Sandoval. We're all trapped right here, like it or not."

Paula called from the kitchen. "We'll be fine then. If the cops can't make it because they're busy with evacuations, then this crazy man who blew up your boat won't be able to call for reinforcements, either."

"Unless they're already here," Reuben said so softly Antonia almost didn't hear him.

Reuben shut down his worry long enough to focus on the practical. Hector was helping Silvio board up the windows on the third story. Paula was cooking something and retrieving all the potted plants from the veranda and balconies. Gavin had gone to make sure all the lower-level windows were secure. None of them could be budged from their duties, arsonist or no arsonist, except possibly Gavin, and he had no choice at the moment. That left Antonia to deal with.

If indeed it was Garza's man who had tried to strand him here, he would not give up because of a storm no matter how intense. Since he could not get Antonia and Paula off the island, they were—to coin a phrase—sitting ducks. Paula would never leave Silvio's side, but he figured Antonia would be safer the farther away she was from him.

He herded her along in front of him on the path to the bungalow, her pace slower than he would like as she picked her way around puddles, ignoring the rain. Antonia was a dreamer, an observer, walking through life as if the world that unrolled before her were meant to be studied and captured in memories or on canvas. He'd loved that about her, but right now, it was driving him nuts.

Along the way she peppered him with questions that he did not answer. Finally, she stopped him with a hand on his chest. His breathing ticked up a notch at the feel of her palm pressed against him. He found his own fingers curled around her wrist.

"It's because of your brother, isn't it?" Her black eyes gleamed, defiant, even in the steady rain. "Whoever that was, he's after you because of Hector."

"That's immaterial."

"No, it's not. Your brother is a criminal, Reuben, can't you see that? He's dragging you down."

"My brother is clean, Antonia. He got out of the business and he's stayed out."

"And you believe that?"

"I believe that. I've prayed every day for the past decade that Hector would go straight, and he has. He was trying to be a good father to Gracie."

"He attacked my sister when she said she was leaving."

"Mia had not a scratch on her. My brother was the one who needed stitches."

"She thought he was going to kill her and take Gracie."

"She thought wrong. Hector loves Gracie, and he knows she needs her mother."

Antonia's eyes flamed, and there was a note of entreaty in her voice. "He went after my sister. She defended herself."

Reuben looked away. There was no time for this again. Not now and he shouldn't have mentioned

Gracie. "Okay, suppose that's how Mia felt. She was scared. She believed she had to defend herself. I get that. Hector has a temper and he loses it sometimes. When Mia was released from jail they could have come to an agreement. All Hector wanted was to see his daughter."

"He's lying about everything, and you're too blinded to see it."

"Your sister is the one breaking the law by snatching Gracie from her father."

She shook her head, eyes hard. "He's a drug runner, Reuben."

"That's in the past, before he even met Mia. He made mistakes and I've forgiven him for that."

She looked away and wiped the moisture off her forehead. "He doesn't deserve your forgiveness."

"Everyone deserves forgiveness, Nee. Didn't you learn that in Sunday school?"

His arrow hit the mark, and she turned on her heel and walked ahead of him on the path, the anger and disappointment simmering between them, thick as the storm-soaked clouds. When they reached the bungalow, he held the door for her and made sure the lantern and flashlight were functioning. He folded the heavy accordion hurricane shutters over the window and clamped them shut. Antonia stood on the porch watching, her long hair swirling in the wind.

"This bungalow is the sturdiest thing we've got.

Hurricane ties, nailed roof. It's all up to code, so I'm optimistic."

"What about the main building?"

Reuben shot a look at Isla, silhouetted against the sky like a grand lady, unaware of the disaster gathering around her. Built in the late 1800s, the beautiful three-story house had been damaged in past hurricanes, and repaired to the best of their ability at the time, but codes and materials had improved since then. There were always other items on the purchase list. He found it ironic that tourists came to Isla to experience a historic setting, yet they required all the expensive modern conveniences from Wi-Fi to flat-screen TVs. Isla was in desperate need of retrofitting, and now it seemed they were out of time. His stomach tightened as he pulled his thoughts back to the bungalow.

"In the small closet there's access to a shelter underneath the bungalow if it looks like it's not going to outlast the hurricane. It will keep you safe from the wind, at least until it floods. Hopefully that won't be for a while. There's water and some food. You'll be okay."

A fresh burst of wind rattled against the shutters. He handed her a second flashlight. "Lock the door and don't open it unless it's me or Silvio."

The fear flickered in her eyes. "You really think someone is coming?"

He didn't want to add to her fear, but he'd always told her the truth and he wasn't going to start lying now. "Yes, I do. Garza wants the island, and he thinks he's going to force me to give it up." He hesitated. "I don't want you involved in this, but I'm worried that you already are."

She sucked in a breath. "The man on the beach and the one on the Jet Ski. You think they were Garza's men?"

"I don't know."

"Why would they think scaring me would influence you? Everyone knows we're not together anymore."

Reuben felt the flood of feelings well up from deep in his soul. *Not together, but you'll always be a part of me.* "Enemies will use anything, even the past. Maybe they thought they could still get to me through you."

Her eyes locked on his. "Can they?"

He wished desperately at that moment that Antonia was still on the side of friend. Of all the things they had been to each other, he missed that friendship the most, the comfort of having someone on his side who knew him completely and loved him anyway. With the rest of the world he'd always had to wonder if friendly folks were cordial as a way to keep on good terms with the Sandoval family or out of fear of his brother.

Past history. Hector was out of that life, though he'd never convince Antonia of that.

"Keep the door locked," he repeated before thrusting a bag into her arms. "Paula made up this food for you."

Antonia blinked. "I thought she hated me."

He shrugged. "She can't stand the thought of anyone hungry."

Antonia sighed. "So I'm supposed to stay shut in here while you fend off this man who just blew up your boats and tried to scare me on the beach?"

"When the police make it here it will all be over. They'll get you back to the mainland."

She took a step toward him, and he saw the beads of water imprisoned, trembling in the strands of her hair like tiny crystals. "What will happen to Silvio, Paula and Gavin while I'm tucked safely away in this bungalow?"

"Nothing."

"How do you know that?"

"Because I'm going to find the guy who blew up my boats before he finds them." *And you.*

Antonia jerked and he thought her face went a little paler, but it might have been a trick of the shadows from the waving palms outside. "Wait for the police. Please, Reuben."

"Won't get anybody here until after the storm."

She toyed with the zipper on her windbreaker. "He'll kill you. You're an orange grower, not a commando."

He saw his own grim smile reflected in the dark

pools of her eyes. "One thing about the Sandovals is they know how to survive."

He waited in the rain until he heard the sound of the lock sliding home.

FIVE

Antonia tried to rest but succeeded only in rolling around on the tiny bed until she couldn't stand it anymore. She reached for her phone and was reminded that she had left it on the dock, tucked safely amidst her art supplies before she came up with the idiotic idea to swim away from the man on the beach.

She tried to find a crack in the hurricane shutters through which she could peer out, but there was none, so she settled for pacing the wooden floorboards. *They thought they could still get to me through you.*

The idea both horrified and intrigued her. She'd been swept into Reuben's world in spite of her deepest desire never to see him again. Then why did it stir in her soul, the thought that he might still care about her? It shouldn't matter. It didn't matter. The past would stay in the past, and if Garza thought she and Reuben still meant something to each other he was mistaken.

She flipped on the small TV and watched dire news predictions about Hurricane Tony. Winds would top 110 miles per hour. Extensive flooding expected. Power outages were certain. At least Mia was safe, somewhere. She wished she could talk to her sister, face-to-face, to see her wide smile and the dimple that showed so often in happier times. Mia refused to tell her where she was, so she would not be further involved. Ironic, since Antonia was now sharing the same island as the man Mia would sacrifice everything to save her daughter from.

The hurricane will pass. I'll get work and save up some money so Mia can find a new life. Someplace. Anyplace. And they would see each other again. She would reunite Gracie with her grandma, too, and it would lift their mother's depression.

A long-staunched flow of guilt surfaced again. Antonia had chosen to follow her passion, to go to art school instead of finding a good, solid mainstream job like the bookkeeping position that was offered to her by a family friend. It was all very well to follow one's passion, until it left you with no steady income and without the means to support a family.

With a sigh, she turned off the TV and peeked into the bag of food, extracting a fragrant rice dish that made her mouth water. She'd forgotten her hunger, but it returned now with a vengeance and she ate every morsel. Stomach full, she lay down again on the bed, staring at a wall, imagining the fresco she could paint there. It would be a panorama of what lay beyond the plaster, the wide Atlantic in the background, the foreground speckled with pockets of lagoon so breathtakingly blue it would dazzle the eye. And there would be a couple there, silhouetted by the tropical sun, hand in hand, delighted with each other and the God-made treasures surrounding them. The girl would have long dark hair and the man, eyes the color of chocolate. An ache settled into Antonia's heart, and she turned her face away and slept.

The walls shook; shutters rattled. Antonia sat up, blinking herself back to reality. Her watch read nearly four o'clock. She pushed the TV power button and found only zigzagging static. The lights still worked, and she turned them on, all of them. She wanted to unfasten those horrible shutters, or even wrench open the front door, but she dared not. Years ago her father had made the same mistake during a much less severe storm, and the damage caused by the wind barreling in was extensive. And then there was the possibility of Garza's man on the loose. She chewed her lip, trying to keep her mind off Reuben and what he might be up to at that very moment.

More out of boredom than fear she decided to explore the shelter that would supposedly save her life if the bungalow was in danger of being swept away. She found the trapdoor in the bottom of the closet and heaved it open. A wave of stuffy, warm air swirled up and tickled her nostrils. A narrow ladder descended into the space, and she held the flashlight down to illuminate the narrow confines. It was small, only about six feet square, she estimated. No exit.

A sharp ringing made her jump. It was the wall phone, an archaic-looking device, which didn't seem to fit in the modernized bungalow.

She picked up the receiver. "Hello?"

There was no answer.

"Who is this?"

Finally, she heard a soft noise. A breath? A whisper? The phone disconnected.

Her stomach contracted and a chill rippled through her. She stood, staring at the phone. The caller knew two very important things: the phone number of the bungalow, which meant it had to be someone on the island, and the fact that Antonia was there, alone, locked in.

Her heart slammed into her ribs.

Slowly she replaced the receiver.

Who knew she was here?

Silvio and Paula. Gavin.

The man who had blown up the boats.

Hector?

She knew he would never give up trying to find

Gracie. The only answer was for Mia to stay in hiding until Hector got in so deep he got himself arrested.

I will spend every penny and every remaining minute of my life until I find Mia, and then she will return to jail for stealing my daughter from me.

Hector knew full well Antonia was imprisoned here in the bungalow.

Cold rippled up her spine.

Perhaps he thought he could scare her into telling him where Gracie was. Or hurt her until she confessed.

Antonia tried to think, ignoring the panic seizing her stomach. Hector couldn't hurt her right here, with Reuben present.

But Reuben might well be off in pursuit of the skimmer captain. Still, she did not think Reuben's brother was the type to get his hands dirty, to do the torturing himself, but he was more than willing to pay people to do it, to rig an explosion that would terrify her and keep her prisoner on the island. Yet the accident might have ended Reuben's life, too. Would Hector murder his own brother to get to her?

But he hadn't known she was on the island; that was unforeseen even to herself. She found that she had wound a strand of her hair tightly around her finger. She exhaled slowly and let it go.

Paranoia. That might be the answer. She'd gone from experiencing the worst earthquake in California's history to finding herself at the center of a howling hurricane. Only a few months before, she'd been there for the catastrophic shaker in San Francisco that trapped her in an abandoned opera house with a killer. Now Hurricane Tony. Disasters could wear on a person.

She wished desperately that she could text her sister, the only way she could get a message to her. Instead she dialed her sister's phone number and left a message, giving her sister both the hotel's main number and the direct line to the bungalow. The storm seemed to be intensifying, from the sound of the wind howling and the pounding of rain on the roof.

Reuben. Was he out in it? Scouring the island for his enemy? The phone was back in her hand before she could talk herself out of it. She wondered as she dialed if he still had the same cell number, the number that she'd been desperate to call so many times since the trial. One ring, two. Was it relief she felt or disappointment? Her finger hovered over the switch hook to disconnect when he answered.

"Antonia?"

"Yes."

"What's wrong?"

Could he still read the tiniest inflection in her voice? The shades of emotion that used to be as clear to him as a Florida sky? She forced a brave tone. "Someone called here. They didn't say anything, just hung up." She felt ridiculous saying it, like a child reporting about monsters under the bed.

He was silent for a moment. "Maybe it was Silvio or Paula trying to call you. Phones are acting up. I'll see if I can check with them."

She thought she heard the sound of palm branches crackling in the wind, but it might have been her imagination. "Where are you?"

"Climbing the Anchor. To get a view of the island."

The Anchor was the remnants of a lighthouse, weathered nearly to ruins, where she knew Reuben and his brother had played for hours as kids. She remembered the sweeping view from the top, Reuben's arm around her and the light in his eyes as he showed her the panorama and told of his childhood exploits like some adult Peter Pan showing off the island to his Wendy.

It's our ocean, Nee. Yours and mine, nobody else's.

Her laughter was snatched up by the wind and then silenced by his kiss, his hands cupping her wind-pinked cheeks, strong and gentle at the same time.

She cleared her throat. "I can't stand being locked up in here."

"It's the safest place."

"But the call…"

"Antonia, you've got to stay put. After—"

The phone went dead and she stared at the receiver in horror.

* * *

Reuben talked on for a moment before he realized that their call had been disconnected. He immediately redialed with no success then called Silvio's cell, which got him Paula for a few seconds before that connection was lost, too. The storm, no doubt, explained why he'd lost Paula, but the bungalow phone should still be up and running…unless the phone line had been cut?

He stood looking up at the relic of a lighthouse, considering. From that vantage point he would be able to see most of the island, what wasn't screened by palms or slash pines. He started up the crumbling stone steps and made it to the sixth before he stopped, turning around.

You're being a fool, Reuben. She's fine.

He was nearly certain it was a phone malfunction and he'd find a calm and collected Antonia pacing the floor.

Still…

As he descended the rocky slope, now slick with rain, he peered toward the main house and saw no comforting glow of light in the windows. Power down. Not unexpected. Silvio would have the generator working soon, if the old thing would cooperate. He chided himself for not purchasing a newer model.

He raced down nearer the beach toward the bungalow. The trail gave him a vantage on the black mangrove islands below, which framed pockets of water ranging in depth from a half mile to five miles. Though it was only a little after five, the sky was nearly dark. The trees, usually teeming with birds, were eerily empty, the water quiet without the smack of feeding trout and redfish or the gentle splashes of the manatees that frequented the lagoon. The creatures all seemed to know that this was no ordinary storm careening toward them. They'd had the good sense to take shelter.

It caught his eye, the shine of metal where it shouldn't be, the odd corner protruding from behind the ruffle of leaves. There for a moment, the concealing foliage was swept aside by the wind and then pushed back into place. He stopped, flopped on his belly and took out his binoculars. There was just enough light left for him to make out the skimmer, revealed for a moment before it was lost again behind the vegetation.

His breath caught. Proof positive. Garza's guy *was* here, on Isla, instead of making a getaway after torching the boats. His pulse beat a tense rhythm in his throat. Now what?

He dialed Hector's number.

"Where are you?" Hector said.

"Near the lagoon. Skimmer's docked here. Are you still at the house?"

"Yes. Silvio is working to get the generator up. The thing is ancient." He paused. "You won't find Garza's man if he doesn't want to be found. He's too well trained for that. Come here, I have a weapon. I can protect you." There was a definite strain in his voice.

Hector could protect him? It felt strange, stacked against all the years Reuben had struggled to shield his brother from his wrong choices. Strange, and comforting that Hector would risk his own life for his older brother, in spite of their past. "I'm the target. Better off not drawing him there."

"He won't know that you're playing the hero. He'd think you'd have the good sense to hunker down inside. Think it through. He's coming here anyway, sooner or later."

Yes, he would be. On the island there were very few places to search. The main building, the boathouse on the far side of the island, a half-ruined lighthouse. His stomach constricted. *And the bungalows*.

He'd made an error sending Antonia out there on her own. He prayed it wasn't a fatal one.

"I'm going to get Antonia. I'll bring her there."

Hector sighed. "Don't do it. She is your enemy, brother."

He didn't reply. After stowing his cell phone, he sprinted up the path that curved away from the lagoon, slipping on the wet gravel. He'd seen tourists jogging on this path and considered it ridiculous. His own job tending the oranges was exhausting physically and mentally. The last thing he'd want to do on vacation was exercise, but it was not the laborers like himself who came to Isla. They were wealthy people who liked to experience roughing it without sacrificing too many luxuries, people like Frank Garza, who ran an empire using a cell phone and probably never left his comfortable chair.

He gritted his teeth. Garza would steal Isla over his dead body.

Just what Garza intended.

His mind followed their reasoning. Break Reuben, and the island would be passed to Hector, who was in no position to argue because he knew what they would do next.

Find Mia. Or Gracie.

Thinking about his niece with her wide grin and big belly chuckle warmed a spot deep inside. "Uncle Booben," she called him and it reduced him to jelly every time. If that little girl asked for a slice of the moon, he'd build a rocket ship to try and get it for her. Maybe someday Antonia could see how much both he and his brother loved Gracie, how much her absence was hurting them.

He sprinted up over the path and down into the hollow that served as some protection for the bungalow. There was no sign of life from the little place, but then, he assured himself, there shouldn't be. The hurricane shutters would make it hard to see any....

Shock reverberated through his body.

The clouds played strange shadows over the tiny front porch. His eyes playing tricks?

No. The door of the bungalow was open, banging in the wind, rain blowing in through the opening.

Reuben felt as if his feet were rooted into the mucky ground. He forced them to move slowly forward until he crept to the front porch, loosening his knife from its sheath. Rain collected in his hair and slithered down the back of his neck, cold, intrusive.

He did not let his brain play out the scenario. If Garza's man had found her...she would have fought. Two summers before, she and Mia were shopping in Miami when Mia's purse was snatched. Her arm was caught in the strap and she went down. He came to find out later that Antonia had chased the man for six blocks and even tripped him once before he got away.

That was the Antonia that Garza's guy would have found.

She would have fought.

But she wouldn't have won.

Not against a mobster.

He wedged his foot against the door and listened. Not a sound came from inside. Knife ready, he sprang through the doorway into the darkened room. No movement, nothing but shadows that confused his senses and made his nerves twitch. He fumbled for the shelf where he knew the lantern was kept and switched it to life.

The tiny place was neat and tidy, no sign of disturbance except for the coverlet, which was flipped askew. A quick look revealed that no one was under the bed. He trained the light downward to the pine floor. A trail of wet patches marked out the passage of wet feet. Man or woman's he couldn't tell. The footprints led to the closet.

Heart thudding, he followed.

Antonia would have hidden in the shelter like he'd told her. There was only one bolt to fasten the hatch from underneath. Easy to kick through. Once inside, there was no exit. She'd trapped herself at his direction.

To his surprise, the hatch was not bolted, nor did it show signs that someone had tried to force it from the outside. He found himself mumbling desperate prayers as he pulled it open.

Something sparkled at him, something dark and viscous, pooling on the floor under the lantern light.

SIX

Antonia held the edges of the wound together to try to stop the bleeding. Her breath came in rasping gasps. There was no pain, not yet, only the sick, strong feeling of terror as she pressed herself against the rough bark of a tree. Rain blurred her vision, and the sudden movement on the porch made her realize someone else was there. She did not recognize the figure until he stumbled out, scanning wildly in all directions.

She scrambled from her hiding place and ran to Reuben.

His face went slack with surprise, and then myriad emotions that were too swift for her to track flitted across his face. Instead of speaking, he sheathed his knife and clutched her to his chest. She felt the mad hammering of his heart. For one inexplicable moment she savored his embrace and breathed in the scent of him.

"I saw blood," he gasped in her ear. "I thought it was yours."

She wriggled loose, sucking in a breath, and held up her hand. "It was."

His face hardened. "Tell me what happened."

She wished he would not look at her face with such laser intensity as she told him. "I heard someone talking, on a radio maybe or a cell phone. I knew it wasn't you because the voice was higher pitched. After a while, he tried the door handle, which didn't open, but he must have had a lock pick because it did after a few minutes." Fear circled her mind again as she recounted it. "I had only enough time to open the closet and prop open the trapdoor to the shelter before I hid under the bed. When the guy came in, I hit him with a lamp, which is how I cut myself. Then I ran."

Reuben seemed to be in the grip of alternating emotions ranging from amusement to horror. "Nee," he said. "Did it occur to you that you might be doing something dangerous? He could have killed you."

"Not with a lamp crashed over his head. I figured it would give me time to get away."

He took a deep breath. "And so it did."

"I hid in the bushes until he came out just a few minutes before you arrived. He talked on the phone again and headed off."

"Toward the main house?"

"No. That way." She pointed toward the far side of the island.

Reuben frowned. "What did he look like, this guy?"

"I only saw him from the back, but he had a slight build and longish hair, I think, down to his shoulders." She broke off. "You look like you know who I'm talking about."

Reuben sighed. "I wish I didn't. His name is Leland. He works for Garza. Some say he's the next in line to run the empire. I think he's the one who came here on the skimmer. Garza wants Isla, so he sent Leland to convince me to sign it over...or kill me if I won't."

Razor-edged fear kicked up inside her. "But this is not the Dark Ages, Reuben. There are laws, even if...even if he did succeed in killing you, he can't just take Isla for himself."

"No, Hector will inherit, and Garza will go after him."

"Hector got himself into that mess," she snapped. "He was Garza's competitor and now he's brought all this trouble to you. He can take care of himself, as far as I'm concerned."

Reuben turned on her, his eyes glowing with anger. "That's not how it works. They go after everyone. That's why you're not safe here, either. Hector refused to pressure me, and Garza knew the best way to get Isla is to come after me and the property will pass to my brother."

"And then I suppose Hector will just hand it over? Why?" she demanded. "For a hefty slice of the pie?

Because he's a mobster even though you refuse to see it."

Reuben looked at the building wall of storm hanging low over the ocean. "Because he'll have no choice."

"Of course he…" The truth struck her silent for a moment. "Gracie," she whispered. "They'll find Gracie." She turned her face to the storm, willing the rippling wind to wash the realization away, but it would not go. Gracie, sweet Gracie caught in the middle. The Sandoval family had sown the seeds of violence for so long and now they had taken root, growing and feeding on greed and power until it threatened to strangle a sweet little girl. Her heart constricted.

"Come on." Reuben took her good hand and guided her along the path. "Let's get you to the house."

She stopped. "And then you're going after Leland. That's a ridiculous idea, Reuben, and you know it."

"I'm not looking to be a hero. I'm going to keep trying the police. Now that we have a name, maybe they'll take it more seriously."

"You can do that from the house."

"I need to know his plans." Reuben shifted. "We're more than likely on our own for days. We'll need some information if we're going to survive that long."

Antonia tried to catch the strands of hair that

whipped at her face, but her wounded hand made it too difficult. "It's a bad plan."

"This from the lamp-crashing girl."

She allowed him a smile.

"It's the only idea I can come up with. As you said, I grow oranges for a living. I don't get much opportunity to practice my cloak-and-dagger routine." His expression softened for the briefest of moments. "I'll call again after I make it to the Anchor and see if he's alone."

"I'm coming."

"No. It's safest in the main house. Silvio will know how to secure the place and Hector…"

"Hector?" Her body stiffened.

He nodded wearily. "I know you hate him, but he can protect you, at least until the police get here or the storm passes, whichever comes first."

"I'll stay with you."

His eyes flared. "You'll slow me down," he said, an edge in his voice. "You're hurt."

She grabbed an edge of the pink T-shirt and ripped off a strip with which she bound her hand, using her teeth to hold the length of the makeshift bandage. "Good to go. Let's get on with it."

His chin went up, rain speckling his forehead. "Antonia, would you listen to reason? Leland is here to hurt or kill me, and standing next to me is the wrong place to be, don't you understand that? You can't help me. You can't make me any safer by forcing yourself into this."

"I'm not helping you. I'm in it because of Gracie. I have to look out for her and my sister, thanks to the Sandovals." She fueled the words with all the darkness that had lived inside her for far too long. They were barbed with anger and tipped with pain, and they found their mark. She saw it in his face, and for the tiniest moment, she felt shame. "Reuben..." she started, but he had already turned and pushed into the undulating waves of nut grass. She heard him talking into his cell phone, relaying to Silvio all that had happened.

"He'll come there. Soon," Reuben said by way of signing off.

Soon.

She zipped her jacket further against the chill that swept through her body.

Reuben tried to rein in his emotions as he shouldered away the wet branches that hung low over the path to the Anchor. He was breathing hard. Antonia's words echoing through his mind. It seemed she was right. They had landed squarely in the middle of this mess because Garza both wanted Isla and hated his brother. Their rancor went deep and wide, circling back to the time some years before when Hector took up their father's mantle and expanded the business, making himself Garza's direct competitor. He might as well have painted a target on his own chest.

One evening, long before Hector met Mia, Reuben had arrived to visit their ailing father, a man who no longer even recognized his sons, and found Hector beaten, lying on the patio, his blood dribbling in rivulets into the chlorinated water. If timing had been otherwise, Hector would have bled to death. God spared his brother's life, and Hector quit the business.

It had taken nearly dying to make him give it up, this lifestyle that awakened a craving in Hector just as strong as the lust for cocaine that fueled the enormous drug trade. It was not the money, the expensive boats and homes. It was the power. Potent and heady, it gripped Hector so strongly it took nearly dying to free him from it. The beating knocked more sense into him than any of Reuben's arguments and downright begging had. And it opened up a new life with room for love and family, the kind he'd found with Mia. God answered Reuben's prayers, and Hector's, too.

Until it all went wrong.

He hadn't noticed anything severe at first—mild depression in his brother, a heightened anxiety maybe. Reuben knew it was in part the difficulty of being purposeless, being unable to find a legitimate business that kept his attention. Hector held to the notion that a man's job was to pay bills and maintain the family, and though Hector had plenty of money, he did not have power or purpose anymore, and it rankled him.

They kept to the path both Reuben and Antonia knew well. It rose in a looping irregular fashion along a route that sloped upward. It would take them to the side of the island where the land met the wide Atlantic, rather than the much quieter stretch that enjoyed protection, sandwiched as it was between Isla and the mainland. It wasn't the most direct route to the lighthouse, but the heavy screen of oak and red bay trees would keep them hidden from Leland, he hoped.

Antonia kept pace behind him. "Is it possible Leland left?" she called. "He doesn't have the element of surprise anymore."

Reuben ducked under a dripping branch, holding it aside for her. "Skimmer's still here. Leland is, too. He's probably got a really bad headache now, though."

She laughed and it thrilled something inside him.

"He deserved a lamp over the head, don't you think?"

"At least."

They emerged from the wood and began a quicker descent down a sandy path. The going was treacherous. Enormous puddles covered the narrow trail, leaving them to slog through as best they could. Antonia lost her sandal in the muck until she was able to fish it out. Reuben felt more acutely the power of the approaching storm, the naked vulnerability of this exposed island. Or perhaps it was their own vulnerability that pricked him.

Something was not right.

Leland had not made much of an effort to pursue Antonia after she bashed him.

Bigger fish to fry, Reuben thought. *You're the primary target, remember?*

Still, he did not imagine Leland was the type to leave a witness unharmed. He stopped again, training a small pair of binoculars along the billowing masses of grass.

"See anything?" Antonia said, closer to him than he'd realized, near enough to feel her hair brush his cheek.

He moved away a pace and pocketed the binoculars. "No, nothing. But something's off."

She sighed. "We're marching up to a ruined lighthouse just before a hurricane hits in search of a mobster. What could possibly be amiss?"

He laughed. "That about sums it up. Let's go."

They approached the fifty-foot brick tower, edging by the ruins of the innkeeper's house, which were now nothing more than a crooked pile of wooden struts. A piece of jagged brick, knocked loose from somewhere above them, fell near Antonia's feet.

"I won't even ask if the Anchor is safe to enter," she said, "because I think I already know the answer."

He knew it, too. The old lighthouse had taken the brunt of violent storms and the long, slow degradation of salt water, which gradually eroded everything but the brick tower and the iron cage at the top. His mother had loved the ancient thing because her father had taken her there often, where she would imagine she was the lighthouse keeper. In turn she had taken Hector and Reuben there, and they had acted out imaginary scenarios of their own. Recently they'd had to board up the doors to keep out curious tourists who might injure themselves.

Reuben found the boards nailed across the door still performing their duty. He searched around for a makeshift tool, finding a flat metal rod that he used to pry out the nails. Antonia took a small flashlight from her back pocket to help him see.

The boards came loose with a squeal, releasing a rush of stale, fetid air. Antonia stepped through and trained her light up into the tower. Crumbling cement steps spiraled upward into darkness. She started climbing immediately and he followed.

They fell into silence, broken only by the sound of their own breathing and the ping of cement fragments grinding under their feet. Abandoned birds' nests clung to the walls and rat droppings speckled some of the steps.

Antonia stopped halfway up. "Catch my breath."

He was grateful as his own heart was hammering. Leaning against the cold brick, he felt the walls shudder occasionally. Would this be the storm that finally toppled the lighthouse? It would be the final irony that the sea would claim this grand lady who had done her part to protect ships from grounding on the shoals. Like his mother, who had left her husband to make a safer way for her sons.

I'm glad you can't see us now, Mom.

He felt Antonia's eyes on him and shook the melancholy thoughts away. "Last fifty steps to go."

His thigh muscles were quivering when they reached the promontory where the Fresnel lens glittered, the panes of glass fracturing their flashlight beam into crazy reflected sparks.

Antonia sucked in a breath. "I forgot about the lens. I always thought it was beautiful, like some massive diamond or something."

"My mother would have agreed. She loved it." He spoke louder over the rush of air whirling in across the iron railings. "There were some collectors who wanted it, but she insisted it belonged here."

He looked at Antonia, her chin cocked, gazing at the broken lens as if it contained all the answers of the universe. How utterly beautiful she was. How he would despise any man who believed himself worthy of her love.

I thought you belonged here, too.

She started to speak, but broke off abruptly.

Following her gaze, he turned to face the Atlantic and words failed him. Across the choppy water, the sky was being consumed in the black maw, a wall of gray broken only by the electric flash of lightning. If there was thunder, he could not hear it over the pummeling wind and creak of the metal promontory.

It was as if both of them, and the island itself, were about to be swallowed whole by a predator like those alien creatures from the science fiction novels he'd devoured as a child. He could not tear his eyes away from the horizon, lost in the last line of an old poem: "And I, cut off from the world, remain, alone with the terrible hurricane."

Antonia reached for his arm. That touch, those long fingers against his skin, felt like the only bit of reality, the one true thing in the entire surreal scenario. He reached for her hand and grasped it, turning away from the storm. He wanted to try for bravado, reassurance, something smooth that his brother would spill effortlessly, a joke perhaps. Instead he savored the feel of her satin skin in his calloused palm. "I've never seen a hurricane this powerful."

She did not pull away. "I haven't, either. We're in trouble, aren't we?"

"Yes," he said simply. "It's too late to get you off the island."

She offered a small smile. "I wouldn't go anyway. You know me. Trouble magnet."

The promontory rocked under a sudden onslaught and she gasped. Without thinking, he pulled her close, pressed her forehead to his mouth and closed a protective arm around her back. "Just wind." He thought she might have sighed.

"What are the odds of escaping a massive earthquake only to run into a hurricane?"

He did not want to speak in case his words would cause her to move away. Unbeknownst to Antonia, he'd contacted her mother when he'd heard about the earthquake and she told him Antonia had escaped unharmed. "Are you scared, trouble magnet?" he asked softly.

"Yes, but at least I can see it coming. Earthquakes just happen. Out of the blue, your world is pulled from under you."

The sensation seemed all too familiar to him. Two and a half years ago he'd been a semi-impoverished orange farmer, rich beyond belief with a woman who loved him, a new niece and a brother on the straight and narrow. Now... He looked again over her head at the monster gaining strength on the horizon, pained when she stepped out of his arms to peer over the iron railing. He was about to lose it all. Again.

"There," she gasped.

He joined her at the railing, noting her hand was clasped so tightly around the metal her knuckles glowed white. She pointed in the distance, to the cove where the boathouse squatted waiting patiently, he'd often imagined, for its turn at restoration.

Only the barest outline of the peaked roof was visible now since the sun had given up and left them to the mercy of the storm. He strained to detect what had drawn her interest. "I don't see…"

A flash of light, there one moment, then gone, shone from one of the three square openings on the lower floor where the boats would be piloted in and secured to the sheltered slips. It was steadier now, small but clear in the gloom.

"What would Leland want in the boathouse?" Antonia said.

Reuben took his binoculars out but was able to add nothing to their meager store of information. "At least it's something to tell the police." At the exact moment he finished giving voice to the thought, another light shone, this time sparkling from the upper level of the boathouse.

SEVEN

Antonia scurried down the staircase after Reuben as fast as she dared. He had his own flashlight out now, and the two beams picked up just enough of the chipped cement to guide them down the spiraling interior.

"Leland's got help," she said, more to make sense of it for herself than to start a conversation.

Reuben grunted something, but she couldn't decipher it. "Where are we going?" she finally managed as they made it to the plywood opening and plunged back out into the rain. She asked again and this time his reply was clear.

"Back to the main house. There's no other choice."

She did not want to return to Isla and Hector, but she could not figure out any other alternative, with the boathouse home to more than one intruder and Hurricane Tony on the way. Truth be told the storm scared her more than she would admit, though she felt it might be a touch of cowardice for a girl who had lived on the ocean to fear a tropical storm turned hurricane.

She'd been eighteen when Charley blasted the area, but instead of battening down with Mia and her parents, she'd been away, struggling to keep herself afloat financially, waitressing and bagging groceries to scrounge up tuition for her first year at art school. Her father had provided her cheerful reports about their condition until the phones had given up, but she remembered the minutes that ticked into hours, wondering if they had made it through unscathed. Later, she learned, her father's boat had been reduced to splinters and part of their roof lost.

She'd finished out the term and gone back for the second before she'd had to quit permanently. Two years of art school would have to do. Her earning power was needed to pay for her mother's doctors' appointments to treat her diabetes and, though her father would never have said it, to supplement his wages as a mullet fisherman after his equipment was destroyed. The large commercial outfits could recover from a hurricane. Men like her father could not.

She blinked back the tingle of unexpected tears. He never had recovered, not really. The fiercely independent man could not provide for his family, and though they eventually were able to buy him another boat, by then he'd lost a few paces both physically and mentally. All her prayers and working part-time jobs and landing the occasional painting contract had not amounted to much, not enough to save him anyway.

She was snapped out of her reverie as they headed once again into the woods and all her powers of concentration were required to keep her footing on the rocky path. Her hand throbbed and her body chilled in spite of the warm Florida temperatures, which even now hovered in the low seventies.

They traveled on for the next half hour, Reuben detouring to the lagoon to examine the skimmer, which was still where it had been tied. There was nothing on board to shed any further light on Leland and his deadly mission, so they alternated walking and jogging back to the main house, arriving near seven o'clock. Reuben used his cell phone to call Silvio, who opened the door for them and then slid the bolt home behind.

A small generator powered a lamp and a camp stove on which Paula was making something that caused Antonia's mouth to water. Hector emerged in the main room, looking annoyingly fresh compared to Reuben, who sat heavily at the table and wiped his face with the towels Paula fetched for them both.

Gavin trotted down the staircase. "You're back. Finally. Thought we were going to have to go out after you. What happened?"

"Have you caught the bad guy yet?" Hector said.

Reuben shook his head. "Too many to catch."

Hector's eyes widened.

Silvio grunted. "More than skimmer guy?"

"They're using the boathouse as a base of operations."

Hector let out a breath.

"What kind of operations?" Paula said, pushing the hair from her face with the back of her hand.

"Yeah, what exactly is going on here?" Gavin said.

Reuben didn't reply.

"They might be waiting out the storm," Antonia suggested even though no one had asked.

"When the storm is over, the police will come," Silvio said. "They'll move before then. I'll try the police again." He squinted at the tiny buttons of his cell phone and finally managed to push the correct keys. After a moment he clacked the phone down in disgust. "Nothing."

Nothing and no one. Antonia could see that the others had reached the same conclusion. They were indeed a very tiny island in the middle of a brewing storm.

Reuben locked eyes with Silvio.

Silvio nodded slowly. "So we wait for them to come."

Gavin's face went slack. "Are you saying there are some mobsters out there coming here to kill us?"

"Not *us*," Reuben said. "Me."

"Why?" Gavin stared at him. "I thought you were

not involved in shady stuff." His gaze shifted to Hector. "Starting up the family business again?"

Hector took a step toward Gavin, who did not back down. "The family is no business of yours."

"Seems to me," Gavin said softly, "that since I almost got blown up and now there are bad guys coming here, it is my business."

Reuben sighed. Gavin was right. "Short version is, Garza's family wants Isla and they've got to go through me to get it. I'm sorry you all got stuck in the crosshairs. If there was any way I could get you out, I would."

Gavin whistled softly. "Should have made my vacation last week permanent. Coming back here might have been a tactical error."

"I'm sorry," Reuben said again. "I'll do everything in my power to fix this mess."

"Yes, that is the only option we have. Hold out until the storm has passed and the cops make it here. Windows are all secure except for the cupola so we can keep watch," Hector said. "Women should stay on the lower floor." He shot a disdainful look at Gavin. "And you, too, I suppose. You'll all be safe there."

"Too late for that," Antonia said. "Leland already found me in the bungalow." She held up her injured hand.

Hector quirked an eyebrow. "And yet here you are.

Safe and sound. So much tougher than my brother gives you credit for. Spine of steel, like your sister."

She started to snarl a reply, but Paula cut her off. "Come here. I'll tend to that hand." Antonia allowed Paula to take her wrist and guide her to the sink. Reuben held a flashlight to add to the weak lamplight while Paula rinsed Antonia's wound with water from a bottle, then added disinfectant from a first-aid kit she'd retrieved.

Reuben patted Antonia's palm with a clean cloth. It made her stomach jump to have her slender fingers in his grasp. Too many memories, too much pain. Still she held her hand steady and did not react.

The touch doesn't mean anything to him, so it shouldn't mean anything to you, she reminded herself. Her mind prodded her with a memory of the two of them, standing together at the top of the lighthouse, staring at Hurricane Tony. She could not fathom the reason why God would have thrown them together once more. If Antonia didn't know Him to be a loving father, she would almost have thought it cruel. Paula applied strips of first-aid tape to the gauze Reuben held to her palm.

Antonia nudged him out of the way and took charge of holding the gauze herself. "I got it," she said. "Thanks."

Paula finished taping and closed the first-aid kit with a snap. "We will not go into the storm shelter unless there is no other choice. Here," she said, thrusting a bowl into Antonia's hands and then Hector's and Gavin's. "Eat."

Hector laughed and took a spoonful of the spicy stew. "Delicious, as always, Paula. Even in the face of disaster, we shall be well fed."

"Don't poke fun," she said. "I know your mother would have done just such a thing."

Hector's face darkened. He put the stew down.

Paula tried to force a bowl upon her husband, but he was busy retrieving a shotgun from a locked safe in the back of the closet. Her mouth opened when she saw it.

"Silvio…"

"After Korea I never wanted to touch a gun again." The weapon trembled slightly in his grip, and he stowed a box of cartridges in his pocket. "Only if I have no other choice," he said to Paula before he put it down and took up his bowl and spoon.

Reuben's mind reeled as he watched the steam rise from the pungent stew. "There's got to be another way," he mused.

Gavin sat next to him. "All right. If I'm going to help in this incomprehensible situation, have you got a weapon for me?"

Hector pursed his lips. "Do you know how to shoot? I would not think a master's program in botany would cover gunmanship."

"My dad was army. He taught me enough." Gavin

cocked his head. "How'd you know I'm studying for a master's in botany?"

Hector did not smile, though his tone was light. "One hears things."

"Yes," Gavin said. "One does."

"Hector has a gun. There's the shotgun." Reuben went to the closet and unlocked the safe, retrieving three sheathed knives, one of which he clipped at his waist. He handed one to Gavin and the other to Antonia. "All I've got."

The knife looked odd in Antonia's hands, as if it carried a weight heavier than its actual mass. She put it down quickly.

Please, Lord. Don't let her have to use it. He tried to force the muscles in his jaw to relax. He was handing out weapons to a grad student and an artist, two people ill equipped to handle violence. Who was he kidding? He himself was an orange grower, not a secret agent or cop or marine. There had been school yard fights, some bruises and even a broken wrist, but nothing that would prepare him for the present scenario.

Gavin contemplated his blade as he removed it from the sheath. "Bringing a knife to a gunfight. Puts us at a disadvantage now, doesn't it?"

Disadvantage is an understatement, Reuben thought as he got up and began to check the windows again, and Gavin took his place next to Paula at the sink, wiping the plates dry after she washed them. The windows were as secure as they'd been the last time he'd checked them, plywood boards still nailed in place, giving the grand hotel the appearance of a derelict tenement building. Would the structure hold? He was not sure. The storm shelter out in the back of the hotel would be their last option.

Since prowling was getting him nowhere, Reuben settled on climbing to the cupola, once he ascertained Hector was safely shut in his room and not inclined to be antagonizing Antonia. He wanted to see if there was any further information to be gleaned. He didn't think there was, but at least it was something to do.

The staircase creaked and groaned under his weight as he fought the tiny door open and stepped into a blast of humid air. The aged wood railings enclosed a small hexagonal space, now puddled with rain and paint chips. A black sky, thick with storm, blotted out any starlight, and even the moon was lost in the darkness.

The door behind him banged. Gavin joined him. They stood in silence for a moment.

"That's one bad-boy storm coming," Gavin said.

"Yeah."

Gavin picked at a paint chip on the weathered rail. "You've got bad boys on all sides, Mr. Sandoval."

Reuben heard the question buried beneath and waited for it.

Gavin ticked off the items on his fingers. "Your

father was a mobster, which is why your mother left, so says the gossip machine. Your brother is a mobster...."

"Used to be. Not anymore."

Gavin paused. "My question is which side did you land on?"

Reuben turned to stare at him, wishing he could see his face more clearly. "Tell me what you're after."

"Is Garza going after you for Isla or because you crossed him?"

"What you really want to know is if I'm in the business."

Gavin nodded slowly. "I guess that's it."

Reuben bit back the tirade that flooded into his mind. "You don't believe what I've told you."

"You have to admit, this isn't exactly your typical island paradise, what with a couple of mobsters on the loose. All seems mighty coincidental to happen to a perfectly innocent guy."

"Some might say," Reuben said, a seed of suspicion taking root into his gut, "it's coincidental that a West Coast college boy decided to get a job here, working in this island paradise, for practically nothing."

"I guess some might."

Gavin did not look quite as young as Reuben had thought. Late twenties? Early thirties? He'd answered a help-wanted ad that Reuben placed in the local paper. Perfectly innocent. Wasn't it?

"My daddy told me you can judge a man by the people who surround him," Gavin said, not smiling now. "You're surrounded by bad dudes."

Reuben felt suddenly that the cupola was very small and the world around it larger than he'd ever imagined. *Bad dudes. Like his brother? Like Gavin perhaps?* "And my dad used to say the most dangerous enemies are the ones who look like friends."

"Yes," Gavin said, voice low. He turned to head back into the house after one more calculating look at Reuben. "Your daddy was right about that."

EIGHT

Antonia wanted to go up to the cupola, to escape the smothering confines of the hotel. She waited for Gavin and Reuben to return. Gavin did, a thoughtful look in his dark eyes, but there was no sign of Reuben. She paced for a while then scratched Charley, who allowed it for a moment before attaching himself to Gavin.

The need to escape grew stronger than her reluctance to be in close quarters with Reuben so she finally headed toward the staircase to the cupola.

Before she made it out of the room, the phone rang, startling everyone.

"It's working again," Paula cried.

"Not for long," Gavin muttered.

Paula answered it, and her face screwed up in thought before she held it out to Antonia.

"It's for me?"

Paula nodded, lips thin. "It's someone named Lulu."

Antonia grabbed the phone. Lulu was her sister's nickname, a secret they'd shared since child-hood. "Lulu?"

"Antonia," her sister said, her voice throaty with emotion. "Are you okay?"

"Yes, I had an accident, but I'm okay."

"Safe from the hurricane?"

The hurricane was not the greater danger at the moment, but she didn't want to upset Mia. "Yes."

"Where are you? Who was that who answered the phone?"

Antonia did her best to explain.

Her sister fell into a surprised silence. "Why are you on Isla?"

Antonia sighed. "It's too complicated to go into now. I'll have to wait out the hurricane here with Reuben, and Paula and Silvio," she hastened to add. She knew she had to tell her sister the rest. She tucked herself into the corner and lowered her voice. "Hector is here, too."

Mia's shock could not have been clearer if she'd been standing in the room. Paula and Silvio had discreetly disappeared into the hallway, and Gavin sat on the far side of the room, fiddling with his cell phone. Even so, Antonia pulled herself to the farthest recesses of the kitchen and squeezed the phone to her ear.

"It's okay," she said. "I'm keeping close tabs on him."

"Stay away from him, please."

"Did you find a place?"

"We managed to get a room to stay in. I watch a woman's children while she's at work. They play with Gracie, so she's okay, but she asks when we can go home and see Daddy and Auntie and Uncle."

Mia was sobbing now in earnest. Pain drove deep in Antonia's chest. Gracie, sweet Gracie.

"It will be okay. I'll get some more money together so you can get a better place," she whispered.

"How can I tell Gracie about her father? How will I ever explain what I did?"

That horrible day replayed itself in her mind. Mia had come to Antonia with her suspicions about Hector—the odd phone calls, the dangerous-looking men who had come to the house, Hector's paranoia underlying a strange and unhealthy energy. Mia was going to leave, take Gracie. She made Antonia promise not to tell Reuben.

And she hadn't.

Instead she'd prayed, gone to the house to help her sister and got there along with the police, who were arresting Mia. Gracie was already sitting in the back of a squad car, her face white, two fingers stuck in her mouth and tears on her cheeks.

It all came out in anguished bits and pieces. Hector had confronted Mia when he found her attempting to leave. He flew into a rage and promised to take Gracie so far away she'd never be found. Then he went after Mia, who stabbed him with a knife their father had owned, a knife Antonia had recently given her sister after she found it in a box of old belongings.

There was no mark on Mia. Not the slightest shred of evidence to connect Hector to crimes of any sort or to prove he'd attacked her. Mia admitted she had gone into the kitchen with the knife when she heard Hector, but only for self-protection. The housekeeper testified that Mia screamed at Hector the night before, threatening to leave him.

Antonia tried to explain it to law enforcement officers. Mia was protecting herself and her daughter. Hector was the criminal. They remained indifferent.

Worst of all was the doubt in the one person Antonia had needed most to believe her—Reuben.

Antonia swallowed hard, lowering her voice as much as she could. "Listen, there's a chance we can find some evidence, something to prove he's in the mob."

Mia sniffed. "No, sis. Stay away from Hector."

If she only knew the current situation.

Mia sighed. "I'm scared."

Me, too. She heard noise in the background.

"I have to go," her sister said. "Please don't take any risks. I can't lose you, too. You're all I have left."

Antonia started to answer, but the phone went dead.

She replaced it in the cradle, looking quickly over

toward Gavin, but he had gone. Even Charley the cat had padded off to some far corner of the hotel. The small lamp glowed on the table, but the gloom overtook it, swallowing up the light. All around, the rain pattered against the covered windows.

Though Hurricane Tony was an act of nature, she knew Hector had brought a storm of his own to the island. "I'm going to survive it, and I'm going to beat you," she whispered into the darkness. *But what about Reuben?* her soul whispered back.

She could not allow herself to consider Hector's brother. He had not believed her about Hector before and he wouldn't now. She was alone. And she would save Gracie any way she could. A noise from the hallway startled her.

Paula stood in the shadows holding a pile of neatly folded blankets. "You're to share our room. Silvio won't want to sleep any time soon. Rest if you can, while the men keep watch."

"I can keep watch," she said. "It's not just a man's job."

Paula shook her head. "They don't want you around, can't you understand that? You tried to ruin the Sandoval family."

"They tried to ruin mine," she cried. "I was protecting my sister." For some reason she desperately wanted this woman to understand why she had given up the one man she loved more than anyone else. The cost was almost too much to bear.

"Reuben was protecting his brother, but you see them all the same, paint them all with the same brush. All the Sandovals are evil in your mind, aren't they?"

Anguish sloshed in her gut. "They are a criminal family who got my sister thrown in jail."

"No," Paula said coldly. "Your sister got herself thrown in jail and she took her child away."

Antonia fought to keep her volume steady. "Tell me the truth. You know Hector is in the business, don't you?"

Paula hesitated, tightening her grip on the bundle in her arms. "I don't know anything."

"Yes, you do. You all know Hector is a criminal, but you protect him and that makes you part of it, and Reuben, too."

Paula spoke so low Antonia had to move closer to catch it all. "Reuben is only guilty of loving his brother. If you can't see that, you never deserved him in the first place." She turned on her heel and moved into the bedroom, throwing the blankets on a small sofa.

"The bed is mine. Rest while you can."

Antonia collapsed on the sofa, her mind spinning in disorienting circles. *You never deserved him in the first place.* Deserved him? Deserved to be with a man blinded to his brother's evil?

She clasped her hands together to pray, but her wild thoughts would not allow it. She settled on alternately pacing and sitting, working through all the details she could remember about her past, their past and what kind of future there could possibly be.

If they survived.

If…

She jerked awake. Minutes later? No, hours, she decided, and the clock confirmed it showing a few minutes after midnight. Paula's bed had been slept in, but she was not there and the door was ajar. Antonia chided herself for falling asleep and tiptoed to the door. The hotel was quiet. She listened, catching the sound of whispered voices from the kitchen.

Padding down the stairs, she paused at the bottom, intending to straighten her hair and rumpled clothing before she intruded on the conversation when she caught one word that stopped her.

"Guilty."

"This isn't the time," Silvio said, his gravelly voice low but unmistakable.

"It may be the only time," Paula answered back. "We're all a part of this now."

"We've been a part of it since we started working for the Sandovals," Silvio said. "Doesn't matter which one. I'm going up to take my turn at watch. I'll talk to Reuben as soon as I can."

"Do you think Hector knows?"

There was a pause. "We can only pray that he doesn't."

"But if he does, Silvio? What if he does?"

"Then there's going to be blood."

Reuben had just returned from a tour of the outside, his clothes were sodden, water running off them onto the front doormat as he let himself in again. Paula would not approve of him leaving puddles, no matter what the circumstances. A carafe of coffee sat on the counter along with ceramic coffee mugs. Paula believed foam cups would be the downfall of modern civilization. Though he wasn't a coffee drinker himself, he was grateful that Paula had managed to make some on the small camp burner. Silvio was enduring the wet misery of the cupola, and the coffee would be a welcome relief.

Gavin was to watch out the front windows through a sliver of a crack between the boards and check the back door. Since there was no sign of the kid, he was probably sleeping somewhere. The thought made Reuben uneasy. Gavin knew more than he should about the Sandovals. Then again, it was nothing that a simple Google search wouldn't reveal. Plenty of material—suspicions, allegations, rumors from back in his father's day. The stuff scandal sheets are made of.

He jogged up the stairs to the cupola. The sound

of snoring mingled with the rain. He pushed through to find Silvio sleeping on a hard wooden chair, shotgun cradled in his arms, mug of coffee perched on the railing.

Sleeping on guard duty? Reuben smiled. He would get much enjoyment from teasing Silvio about that.

"Hey, old man. Wake up or it's K.P. duty for you."

Silvio grunted but did not rouse. Reuben shook him more forcefully with no better result. Breath quickening, Reuben shone his flashlight at Silvio, whose face was completely slack. He bent down and slung Silvio firefighter style over his shoulder and carried him down to the lobby, depositing him gently onto the sofa. He called for Paula, who came immediately, still dressed. Antonia followed, also fully dressed, rubbing her eyes.

Paula let out a cry when she saw Silvio and dropped to her knees at his side. "What happened?"

"He's asleep, but I can't wake him." Reuben checked Silvio's pulse and found it steady and strong. "Heart's okay, I think." Reuben paused. "He was drinking coffee."

Antonia locked eyes with his. Then she went to the kitchen and peered into the top of the carafe. "Reuben, there is some residue at the bottom. Pills, I think."

Paula's face cracked. "He's been poisoned."

"I think just drugged. Sleeping pills probably."

He squeezed Paula's hand. "He's going to be okay after he sleeps it off."

Paula nodded, blinking back tears, and stroked Silvio's hand.

Reuben joined Antonia. "Did you drink any coffee?"

She shook her head. "No, and I guess Paula didn't, either. You?"

"I'm not big on coffee but…" A thought struck him. "Gavin is." He went to the bottom of the staircase. "Hector, Gavin," he shouted. "Come down here."

There was no answer. He took the steps two at a time to reach the tiny bedroom at the top of the stairs, the one Hector had claimed. Not bothering to knock, he shoved his way through.

The bed was neatly made. Dread rippled through his insides.

"Do you think Hector drugged the coffee? Or Gavin?" Antonia said.

"Why would either one of them do that? We could have all had it and left ourselves helpless."

"And at the mercy of Leland and Garza's men," Antonia finished.

Reuben sprinted past her, grabbing his flashlight from the kitchen and heading for the back. He threw open the door, fresh air bathing his face.

Reuben readied the flashlight. The floor was spattered by the rain intruding through the open door, banging in the wind. He played the flashlight around outside, Antonia doing the same. Nothing. No sign of Gavin, either.

He peered into the lashing rain. Had his brother gone this way to enact some sort of plan?

Had Gavin?

He turned to Antonia. "They're both gone."

"Why would Gavin leave?"

Reuben shook his head. "I have no idea."

They heard the sounds at exactly the same moment; one pierced through the sound of the storm, then two more.

"What…?"

Reuben didn't answer as he sprinted into the storm toward the sound of the gunshots.

NINE

Not allowing herself to consider the stupidity of her actions, Antonia ran after him. Perhaps it was the lingering shadow of their years together that pushed her to follow Reuben anywhere in any circumstance. Nature seemed to mirror their past as the storm shoved her along with such force it felt as if she was fighting against an assailant. Driving rain, nearly horizontal now, slammed into her in stinging needles. Fumbling for her light, she flicked it on, the beam picking out rain shrouded cabbage palms nearly bent double. Moonlight flickered through the clouds and then disappeared, advancing and retreating as if teasing them.

She realized with a start that she could hear nothing but the storm and that she was alone. Dancing shadows made her twitch as she imagined the shooter, whoever it was, taking a bead on the back of her neck.

Reuben had vanished into the trees just to her

right and she followed, grit sticking to the bottom of her shoes.

"Reuben?" she whispered. Ridiculous, as he wouldn't be able to hear a thing over the pelting rain, but there was a gunman nearby. She was not familiar enough with guns to know how close the shooter had been. Close enough to kill Reuben, she thought, stomach convulsing.

She stepped over a fallen tree, landing ankle-deep in water. To her right, what used to be a ribbon of creek bisecting the island on its way to the lagoon was now wide and rushing, adding to the cacophony. A flicker of movement ahead told her Reuben had stopped at the edge of the creek. She caught up as he bent under a thick tangle of dripping branches.

"What…?" she started to say as loudly as she dared until he shook his head in warning.

"Go back," he said, gesturing toward the house.

She shook her head. "I'm staying with you."

"I—" He paused as two bodies came crashing through the foliage. Leland thrashed through a clump of bushes, and two seconds later, Hector followed, throwing himself at Leland's ankles, sending him sliding across the slick wire grass.

Reuben leaped toward his brother to assist, but Leland had made it back to his feet and whirled to face them. "Come on, Reuben," Leland shouted above the rain. "Let's dance. Mr. Garza wants his island." He smiled, a ghastly grimace in the darkness, hands loose and ready for a fight, watch glinting in the snatches of moonlight.

Antonia's stomach dropped as she finally got a good glimpse of Garza's man. Though she'd only gotten a quick impression before, she felt sure he was the same person who had followed her from the airport, the man with the gold watch who called the guy on the Jet Ski to collect her. Or watch her drown, she wasn't sure which. He'd broken into the bungalow when his earlier plans hadn't worked. The realization stunned her to the point where she almost missed what unfolded.

Reuben launched himself forward until Hector reached out a hand and caught his brother on the shin, bringing him to the ground so hard she heard the breath come whooshing out of him. Pushing through her stupor, Antonia stumbled in to help when Leland darted forward and grabbed a handful of her hair.

Pain shot through her head as he yanked her close. "While the boys are busy playing around, you can come along with me. We've been waiting for you."

She clawed his fingers, trying to pry them loose, and kicked out, but could not make contact and maintain her footing. "Get your hands off me," she spat.

"Not likely," he said with a laugh. Letting go of her hair, he took her wrist and dragged her away from Reuben.

Heart hammering as hard as the rain that pelted down around them, she allowed herself to be carried along a few steps while she calculated her best means of escape. Wet branches slapped at her face as Leland plowed along. His grip never loosened, so she waited until he maneuvered over a fallen log. Once he stepped up, she snapped her wrist in the direction of his thumb and fingers, the weakest point, and she came loose from his grasp, scrambling backward.

Leland let out a growl and surged forward. "Naughty, naughty."

She had already sprinted away, slipping and sliding, breath coming in frantic gasps as she felt him close the gap. She could hear him slap aside the foliage, twigs snapping as he neared.

Faster, faster, her mind screamed into the rain. She turned to see him just behind her, his fingers grazing her shoulder, eyes widening as he caught sight of something that made him pull to a stop. He muttered a string of words, which she could not hear, and gave her a jaunty salute.

"Later then, *señorita*." He grinned and sprinted off into the darkness just as Hector and Reuben hurtled into view. They reached her within seconds.

Reuben grasped her forearms, breathing hard. "Did he hurt you?"

"No," she said, sucking in a breath.

He looked as if he didn't believe her, his fingers

clutching her closer until she was pressed against his chest. "Are you sure?" he whispered raggedly into her ear.

She closed her eyes and some part of her relished the need she heard there, the echoes of love long past, tender and bittersweet. "I'm okay," she murmured. *I'm okay until you let go,* her fickle heart finished. Where had that secret whisper come from? A place that had sealed over long ago. She pulled away, restoring her powers of reason.

Hector had jogged past them and now he returned, panting hard. "Can't find him. He's headed back to the boathouse. I'm going to cut him off."

"No," Reuben yelled over the storm. "You're going to tell me what happened. We heard shots."

Hector started to reply when a branch broke loose in the howling wind and spiraled toward them. Scampering into the trees, they avoided the pinwheeling branch as it crashed by.

"Let's get back to the house," Reuben yelled. "We'll talk there."

Hector nodded, and they made for the hotel, though Antonia was so disoriented by the storm and Leland that she was not sure in which direction they were traveling. Wind tore at her clothes and nearly took her off her feet more than once. Her inner thoughts were just as disconcerting as the storm.

We've been waiting for you.

Why her? She had no connection to Isla, not anymore. Was Reuben right? She was to be used as a bargaining chip against him? A feeling of dread seemed to have lodged itself deep inside, and she could not shake the idea that she was a part of a game where she didn't know the rules, hadn't even known she was playing.

As they approached the bend that marked the last quarter mile back to Isla, Reuben tripped over something and went to his hands and knees. He jerked backward so quickly Antonia thought he must have been bitten by a snake. Recovering quickly, he knelt again, posture stiff with shock.

She bent closer and saw for herself. A man's feet protruded from the shrubbery, the white stripes on the leather sneakers shining unnaturally in the darkness. Horror filled her every pore. She sank next to Reuben, who pulled the body from the shrubs and began searching for a pulse.

"He's alive," Reuben said, rolling him over.

Antonia gasped. Gavin's eyes were closed, a trickle of blood oozing from a cut on his cheekbone.

Reuben shone his own light along Gavin's torso, locating the bullet hole in his windbreaker. "We have to get him back to the house. Hector—" He looked around wildly. "Hector!" His shout echoed through the rain-soaked night.

Though Reuben continued to yell, Antonia knew it was futile.

Hector was gone. Maybe he'd decided to go after Leland on his own.

She looked down at Gavin's slack face.

Or maybe he was running away from what he'd done.

Reuben knew his priority had to be the wounded man, though his stomach stayed tied into painful knots as he lifted Gavin free from the branches. Antonia shone her flashlight along the ground, alerting him to obstacles. Even with the light, they stumbled many times, and Reuben nearly lost his grip on Gavin's limp body. The trees offered some shelter, but they were still battered by wind and rain.

As they staggered on, Reuben figured Antonia was asking herself the same questions he was. Who shot Gavin? And where was Hector?

Reaching Isla, Antonia helped Reuben get Gavin through the narrow door before shutting and bolting it behind them. Reuben, panting hard, made his way arduously through the kitchen until he reached the lobby, where Paula was patting the hand of a groaning Silvio.

Her mouth fell open as Reuben explained that Gavin had been shot.

Paula had enough presence of mind not to pepper him with questions, instead grabbing the first-aid kit and following Reuben to the settee, where he laid the younger man down. She unzipped his jacket and pushed up his shirt to expose the bullet wound and then rolled him slightly to check the exit point.

"I think it missed the vital organs and passed clean through, fortunately for him." Antonia looked impressed as Paula applied pressure to the wound until the bleeding slowed and taped bandages neatly in place. She caught Antonia's expression.

"I used to help my father. He was a country doctor, and you wouldn't believe some of the situations he dealt with."

Reuben fetched a towel, which Paula used to dry Gavin's face and hands, and Antonia handed her a blanket to drape over him. "Where's Hector?" Paula said.

"Out in the storm," Antonia told her.

Paula frowned, considering, until Silvio groaned again from his prone position on the sofa and she got to her feet to tend to him, mumbling something about being an innkeeper, not a charge nurse.

Reuben bent over Gavin and checked his pockets. "No ID."

"Why would he have some on him? He's your gardener, isn't he?"

Reuben looked down at Gavin's face. "I'm beginning to wonder." He removed Gavin's cell phone and tried to thumb it to life, but he could not get past the password required.

Antonia leaned close. "Who do you think shot him?"

"Not my brother," Reuben snapped. "Leland, Garza's guy, did."

"He didn't seem to have a gun." Antonia twirled a strand of her hair tightly around her finger. "Otherwise, he could have just shot us all out there."

He had no answer for that. Antonia hesitated; there was something she was not telling him. "What?"

"It was definitely Leland who followed me from the airport and sent the watercraft." She shook her head. "It seems ridiculous to think they could get to you through me."

"They must have heard—known—how much I loved you." The words seemed to cut their way out of him. Loved. Past tense. Past, but so powerful Garza knew that Antonia still held sway over his heart even if they couldn't be together.

Antonia looked at him for a long time before she turned away. "What a waste of effort. They don't know that I'm not in your life anymore."

Not in my life, but always in my heart, in my blood, in the memories that keep me hanging on when there's nothing else. No one else. "I'm sorry, Nee. This never should have happened." He closed his eyes and sighed. When he opened them, he felt tired and worn. He pulled out his phone and texted, chewing his lip waiting for a reply that didn't come. "No answer from Hector. He's in over his head." He expected a cutting remark from her, indicating Hector had gotten what he deserved.

Instead, her hand found his. "I'm sure he'll be okay."

His pulse throbbed. "Thanks." He held on to her and felt the warmth return to both of them. "I'm going to get you out of this, Nee. I promise."

She smiled. "I know you'll give it your best shot." She pressed his fingers to her lips, and the kiss trailed life back into his body. The old sparks danced inside, though he fought hard to keep them down.

She let go and picked up the rotary phone receiver on the kitchen wall, replacing it when she heard no dial tone. "I'll try again later."

"Hurricane is here," Reuben said. "We're on our own."

The words seemed to linger in the dark room.

Antonia hugged herself. "So we wait."

With a gunman outside and two men incapacitated.

TEN

Reuben frowned. "I'm going to look in Gavin's room. Maybe he stashed some belongings there."

"How's that going to help?" Antonia said, following.

"Probably won't do anything but keep us busy for a few minutes."

"Then that's enough reason for me," Antonia said.

"Are you going up there dripping wet?" Paula called. "What will it do to the floors?"

Reuben gave her a wry smile. "Paula, in a few hours we may not have any floors left."

She shook her head and crossed the room to check on Gavin.

Gavin's room was actually a tiny alcove that housed a library and study. The walls were lined with books—Reuben's mother's, she knew—volume upon volume about ornithology and shell collecting, several hefty tomes of collected poetry and a half dozen ragged Bibles. A delicate desk was pushed against one wall to make room for a sleeping bag, which was folded neatly on the floor along with a pillow Paula had rounded up for Gavin.

Gavin's pack was nowhere to be found.

"If he was going out into a hurricane, wouldn't you think he'd take his pack?"

"Maybe he did and the shooter took it or it's lying there in the bushes somewhere and we couldn't see it."

"I still don't see why Hector and Gavin were both out in the storm in the first place. One followed the other?"

Reuben's eyes narrowed in thought. "I can see my brother sneaking out, thinking he's going to save us all and put a dent in Leland's plan."

"And Gavin followed him? Why?" Antonia recalled the conversation she'd heard earlier between Silvio and Paula.

Do you think Hector knows?

She shivered, recalling Silvio's last words.

Then there's going to be blood.

"Paula knows something about Gavin." She watched him start visibly. "I think you'd better talk to her."

He jerked, eyes darkening. "Paula and Silvio are my friends, like parents. They wouldn't hide anything from me."

Antonia hoped that he was right as she followed him back down the stairs. Paula sat calmly on a stuffed ottoman, the two unconscious men on either side.

"Find anything?" she asked.

"No." Reuben sat opposite her on the sofa, leaning forward with elbows on his knees to look her squarely in the eyes. "Do you know something about Gavin, Paula?"

Paula folded her arms. "Why would you ask that?"

Antonia spoke up. "I heard you talking to Silvio. You said there would be blood if Hector found out. What were you talking about?"

Paula gave Antonia a look of disdain. "Eavesdropping, were you?"

Reuben held up a hand. "Don't stall. Do you have any information?"

She pursed her lips. "Silvio said we shouldn't tell because we weren't sure. He didn't want to get anyone in trouble...or killed."

"We're past that. You have to tell me." His tone was stern, but he gathered up her hand in his. "I know you would never keep information from me unless you had a good reason. I need to know what's going on, and Silvio would agree if he was awake."

"I love you, Reuben," she said, "and you know I would do anything for you, but Silvio is my husband and I will stand by his wishes."

Antonia watched the feelings flicker across Reuben's face like waves tumbling over the sand. Affection, exasperation, respect. "Paula, I love you, too," was all he said, before pressing a kiss on her wrinkled brow.

That one tiny gesture awakened a flood of respect for Reuben. Even with the stakes mounting higher every second, he would not force Paula to do anything.

Pink cheeked, Paula stood up and checked on Gavin's wound, replacing the bandage with swift and skillful fingers.

Reuben watched, face drawn in painful contemplation.

Antonia knew that whatever Silvio had to tell them would change everything. She moved next to Reuben. "What are you thinking?"

"I'm thinking Silvio needs to wake up. Soon. I need to know the truth about Gavin."

"Maybe the real question is not who he is," she said quietly, "but who shot him."

He rounded on her. "It was not my brother, not unless Gavin was threatening his life or mine." He headed for the back door.

"Where are you going?"

"To see if he dropped his pack outside."

"And if you run into Leland?"

"I won't. He's probably gone to meet up with his guy at the boathouse."

"I'll help you look."

"No, I need you to help Paula move all the food

and water she can find to the storm shelter. We need to be prepared."

She was going to protest, but his eyes kindled with fire. "Look, Nee. I can't do this alone. You have to help me, and right now that means making sure we have enough supplies to outlast the hurricane. Get some rest if you can." He huffed out a breath and gentled his voice. "Please do that for me."

It was the quiet tone, the ribbon of worry infusing the words, that struck her, cutting loose a wave of tenderness that she had not known still existed deep down inside. He could not order her to do anything, but if he asked in that sincere way, she could not refuse him.

"Reuben, I will always do what I can to help you." She added quickly, "As a friend."

His smile was bitter. "If we just weren't so busy being enemies."

They locked eyes for a moment, and Antonia felt again the ache that took root deep down when he had defended his brother, the criminal who would ultimately destroy Reuben. She was sure.

She pulled back and watched him disappear into the shadowed staircase. Fatigue slowed her steps as she returned to Paula, who was bent over a restless Silvio. "He'll be awake soon," she said, more to herself than Antonia. Straightening, she marched into the kitchen. "Reuben is worried the roof will go. I think he's wrong, but we'll move supplies to the storm shelter in case he isn't."

"He's wrong about a lot of things," Antonia grumbled.

Paula began to pull cans of food from the kitchen cupboard and put them into a cardboard container. "Do you have two parents who love you?"

Antonia started. "Yes, I did. My father passed."

"Well so did Reuben, and they're both dead now, too, but he had to choose between them, two people who loved him to distraction."

"His dad was a criminal."

Paula continued to load the box. "Criminals can love their children, too. Reuben went with his mother, and it broke his father's heart. When he turned eighteen, Hector went with his father, and it broke his mother's heart."

Antonia considered how it would be for a child to have to choose between his parents.

She felt Paula's gaze on her. "I loved Reuben's mother. She was the child I never had. I saw what it cost her to take the boys out of that life, and I witnessed what it cost her to see one return. She never stopped praying for Hector. 'No storm's too big for God,' she'd say, and she made sure Reuben believed it also."

An uneasy feeling stirred in Antonia's belly. She believed it, too, that no one was beyond redemption, or did she? Had the hurts and disappointments caused her to stop believing the truth that God was big enough to change even the darkest heart?

Accepting the two gallon jugs of water that Paula handed her, she started for the back door when a groan stopped them both.

Gavin grunted as he heaved himself upright, eyes wild and mouth tight with pain.

"Where are they?"

Antonia and Paula put down their burdens and hastened to stop him from trying to stand. They were too late; Gavin hauled himself to his feet. "Where is he?"

"Who?" Antonia pressed. "Hector?"

"He's gone away," Paula said soothingly.

"They'll kill him," he moaned, eyes abruptly becoming unfocused as he collapsed to the floor. Antonia caught him by the arm and broke his fall.

Paula muttered as she took hold of his legs, and they maneuvered him back up onto the sofa. She checked his wound. "Started the thing bleeding again. Bring me a clean towel from the drawer."

Antonia ran to fetch the makeshift bandage, and Paula wrapped the injury again.

Though she desperately wanted Gavin to come to again and explain himself, his eyes remained stubbornly closed.

They'll kill him.

Was he speaking about Hector? Or Reuben?

The clock read two-thirty in the morning. The hurricane was due to make landfall within hours.

Hurry, Reuben.

Reuben spent a fruitless half hour pawing through wet shrubbery along the rain-slicked path. He noted with growing alarm that the creek was now more than half full. If Tony dropped any more than ten inches, the rain would overflow the banks and likely submerge the ground floor of the Isla Hotel.

He marveled again at God's incredible power to change the tiny plans of men with one strong blast of weather. On his twenty-acre organic farm on the mainland, he'd learned to stave off frost damage by spraying the fruits with water to form a protective barrier of ice, which would hover just at the freezing point. He'd managed to hang on to a few good workers to help him with the laborious hand picking and ripped out rows of precious trees planted by his uncle when they contracted citrus greening disease. Not once in all the struggles did he consider quitting. It was in his blood since the moment he visited his uncle's orchard for the first time, and he considered himself blessed to be able to bring something out of the earth with God's help.

But hurricanes were different. His relatively young Seville oranges, bitter and thick skinned for marmalade, would be decimated by the wind. Maybe the older trees…the Valencias…

No way, Reuben. You're going to kiss this year's crops goodbye. Deal with it.

He would. Somehow, he would start over.

A branch snapped loose from a tree and skimmed by his feet.

But how would he keep Isla going if she did not survive the storm?

The Lord giveth.

His stomach clenched as he pictured Antonia's face.

And He taketh away.

He gritted his teeth and shone his flashlight into the shrubbery. She wasn't his to lose anymore; it would be enough to keep her alive.

Soaked in spite of his jacket, Reuben tried to figure out which direction Gavin would have taken. He could have headed up the small hill on the path toward the Anchor, but considering where Reuben had discovered him lying, he figured the man took the river path…the same direction from which Hector had emerged.

His eyes played tricks on him as the foliage danced and rolled. He wished he could risk another trip to the Anchor to keep tabs on Leland and his men or go after his brother, but he dared not leave Antonia and Paula unprotected.

His brother or Antonia. The choice had ruined them before.

Disheartened, face stinging from the pelting rain,

he started the return trip to Isla when he saw it—the strap of Gavin's backpack, caught by a branch. He rooted around in the shrub until he extracted it. Feeling like Jason finding his golden fleece, he hurried as fast as the wet path would allow back to the hotel.

He slammed inside, arriving just as Silvio sat upright, eyes bleary.

Antonia and Paula stood next to him.

"Is he okay?" Reuben said.

"'Course I'm okay. Musta dozed. Getting old."

"You had help," Paula said. "Someone put sleeping pills in the coffee."

Silvio began to mutter angrily, brushing aside the cup of water Antonia offered him and trying to get to his feet. "Aww, stop clucking around me like a bunch of hens. I'm fine."

Paula laughed. "So you are."

Reuben held up the pack. "Gavin's been shot. I found his pack outside in the rain."

Silvio's skin blanched. "Oh, no."

"Tell me, Silvio. What do you know about Gavin?"

"Didn't know anything for sure. Wanted some proof before I went blabbing accusations all over."

Reuben used his last bit of self-control to refrain from barking questions.

Silvio ran a hand over his weathered face. "Last night, while everyone was scurrying around boarding up windows, I went to the shed to get some oil for the lanterns. Gavin was out there, talking on the phone, and he didn't see me coming."

"Talking to whom?"

"Not sure, but I thought…"

Reuben's stomach tightened. "You thought what?"

Paula blurted out the words. "He thought that Gavin was talking to his boss."

"What kind of boss?" Antonia asked.

Silvio coughed. "He said *sir* and *investigation*."

The words fell heavily and left a silence in their wake. "He's a cop?" Antonia ventured finally.

Reuben flopped on the couch, his head falling against the back, eyes closed. He let out an enormous sigh. "Probably DEA. I should have known. Why else would a guy like that want to work here?"

Antonia fisted her hands on her hips. "It makes perfect sense. He's been working here for months trying to gather information about your brother or maybe to find out if you're working with him. Hector is dragging you into ruin," she snapped. "Your loyalty to him will destroy you, Reuben. What's it going to take for you to see that?"

He jerked upright, eyes flashing. "I love my brother just like you love your sister, and I'm not going to believe he's back in the mob."

"He's a criminal, and he has no right to involve you."

Reuben stood. "And so are you, Antonia, because

you helped your sister kidnap my niece. Did you have the right to do that?"

The tension crackled between them until he broke away and grabbed the backpack. "Let's see what our spy packed for the trip," he said bitterly. The pack was wet but the inside still relatively dry thanks to a nylon lining. Dumping the pack out onto the table, he found ammunition for a gun that wasn't there.

"He had more to bring to this shootout than the knife you gave him," Silvio grumbled, holding on to Paula's shoulder for support.

Reuben extracted the knife he'd loaned Gavin and pocketed it.

"If Gavin is undercover, then the cops know Hector is here, and Leland, too," Antonia said.

Reuben felt a stir of hope. If the cops knew the situation, they would get backup here for their agent as soon as they could. He reached deeper into the backpack. Gavin's wallet did not prove to be of much help. The driver's license indicated his name really was Gavin Campbell, but there was no identification to show he was working for law enforcement. Reuben threw the bag down in frustration when he heard an odd thunk. He looked again and discovered a small metal rectangle shoved in a pocket he hadn't noticed before.

The bottom had an output jack. It was a recording

device. "He chucked the microphone somewhere." Reuben stared at the tiny machine.

"What was he recording?" Antonia said.

Reuben's nerves jumped as he pressed the play button.

They leaned forward to listen. At first it sounded like nothing more than the rumbles of a storm, the audio crackling with noise. Reuben turned the volume up all the way.

"...all off. We got cops involved now." It was Hector speaking.

"You don't get to decide."

"Listen, Leland," Hector said, voice louder, insistent.

The voices were swallowed up in storm noise until a few seconds later.

"Too late," Leland said. There was a pause. "...saw something."

The sounds became hurried, branches snapping, and then the click indicating the end of the tape.

Reuben swallowed. "He stowed the device and took off when Leland spotted him."

"Right before he got shot," Silvio added.

Reuben played the tape again, and they listened in silence.

Paula chewed a nail nervously. "What does 'all off' mean?"

Reuben did not want to answer the question, did not want to face the import of those two little words.

"It means my brother had some sort of deal going with Leland." He turned to look at Antonia. "And you were right all along."

ELEVEN

She should have felt justified, satisfied, thrilled that Reuben had finally been forced to face the truth about his brother. Instead, as she looked into his stark face, drinking in the grief in his brown eyes, she felt only compassion. The mirror she'd held up to Hector had reflected back a criminal, but it also cast a dark shadow on his brother's faith. "Reuben," she said softly. "I'm sorry."

"And why would you be sorry?" he said in a tone that made something chill deep inside her. His eyes were flat and cold. "It's what you've been saying the whole time. Your sister is right. You're right. My brother is a criminal, and I've been blind, stupid and naive."

She opened her mouth to answer, but nothing would come out.

Paula reached out a hand to Reuben. "We don't know what he was up to."

"Doesn't matter," Reuben spat. "If it involved Leland, it's bad. Bad enough to bring the cops here."

Paula looked helplessly at Antonia and Silvio, as if she were searching for something comforting to offer. She found nothing and pressed a knuckle to her mouth.

Reuben spun on his heel. "Going to the cupola."

"I'll go, too," Silvio said.

"No," Reuben said. "See to the shelter. Storm's about to hit. If we lose the hotel, our best chance of survival will be in there. Silvio's made it his mission over the years to reinforce the walls and upgrade the roofing to meet code. We should prepare a bed of some kind there for Gavin." He trudged up the steps, and Antonia watched until he was out of sight.

She found Paula staring at nothing. "This can't be true. Hector has goodness inside him, deep down." Tears glimmered in her eyes.

Silvio squeezed her around the shoulders. "We don't know what happened. Maybe when Boy Cop wakes up, he can fill in the gaps. Jumping to conclusions ain't going to help anyone, is it?" He gathered her into his chest and kissed her wrinkled brow. "Okay now. Time to get going. I'll haul the supplies to the shelter. Don't want you ladies outside with—" he paused "—with bad guys and a storm. Pile up everything that needs to go and stack it in the kitchen."

Antonia held the door for Silvio as he hefted several gallon jugs of water and plunged out into the rain. Paula packed up a bag with bandages, shaking her head all the while.

Antonia's mind was not on the survival details. She couldn't stop thinking about what had happened. She'd gotten the thing she'd longed for and prayed about. Hector was crooked and Reuben could see it at long last. Yet it was not triumph, but grief or perhaps guilt that clawed at her chest. She realized suddenly that she had not been praying for Hector's salvation, but for his conviction. She'd wanted him to fall and now he had. The thought shamed her.

"Here," Paula said, piling sofa cushions into her arms. "The shelter is small, no room for a cot. We'll have to lay Mr. Campbell down on the cushions."

Silvio was already struggling through the rain with a box containing bread, peanut butter and other foodstuffs, so Antonia shoved out into the storm, her arms laden with pillows. The wind nearly took her off her feet, but she managed to both cling to the cushions and hunker over them to keep from going over backward. Struggling forward, she pressed on, nearly blinded by driving rain until Silvio grabbed her elbow and guided her into the shelter, where she stood panting.

"Didn't I tell ya to stay in the house?" he grumped.

"Yes, but I don't listen very well."

He stared for a moment, then let loose with a gravelly laugh. "At least yer honest about that. Well," he said, sweeping an arm around the six-by-ten-foot space. "This here's the island of safety on this island of danger." He laughed again at his joke.

She took in the thick walls, the low roof, the exposed plywood and beam interior. One small window, double paned and covered by a storm shutter, and the door were the only entrances and exits.

"Reuben's mama insisted we always keep the shelter up to snuff, even if there wasn't money to treat the main house the same."

"Did you build it?"

"Mostly," he said. "Reuben helped right alongside me, but he ain't much of a carpenter. Started it way back when his mama brought the boys here. Hector helped, too, some. He's not bad with a hammer and nails. Could have been a good line for him if he'd pursued it." Something shimmered in Silvio's eyes.

"You love them, don't you? Reuben and his brother."

"Ah, I've known them boys since they were born. Mr. Sandoval hired me to work on his boats 'cause we served together in the navy. Reuben was always easy, loved boats, loved the sun, loved people and the ocean, most of all loved working in his uncle's fields. Didn't ever see a boy so completely content working the earth. But Hector, he was different. I never really understood him. He needed something, power, maybe, or importance. Dunno. Maybe it was the same craving that got its hooks into his father. He was a good man once upon a time. I know because he saved my life." Silvio turned his gaze on

Antonia. "One thing I can tell you, Hector loves his daughter."

Antonia's breath caught thinking about little Gracie. "My sister was trying to protect her."

His eyes fell. "I was, too, but I wonder if I destroyed Hector and his family while I was at it."

"I don't understand."

His face seemed to age before her eyes, grooves deepening around his mouth and the skin of his jaw slackening. "I was at the house that day. Couple of Hector's men were having trouble working on one of his boats. I went to help. Was in the kitchen grabbing some water."

"What day?"

"Day it happened."

She felt the tingle of approaching dread. "Silvio, what are you saying?"

"I heard Mia talking on the phone, to you I suppose it was, saying she was going to take Gracie and leave."

Her mouth went dry. "And you told Hector."

His eyes blazed for a moment. "He's the man. It's his job to hold the family together." His voice faltered. "I said he should go talk to her, apologize for whatever idiotic thing he did, make amends and do anything he could think of to straighten it out. I didn't know… How could I know?"

"That Hector would go after her and she'd stab him?"

Silvio let out a slow breath that seemed to leave

his shoulders hunched. "I thought it would help. Man's got to keep his family together. I never imagined Hector would lay a finger on Mia."

Antonia felt sick. None of them had escaped the shadow of that terrible day. "You couldn't have known."

"Don't matter. Important thing is for you to know Hector loves Gracie and whatever dumb things he's done or is doing don't change that one little bit. He's her daddy and he loves her."

Antonia thought about her sister, alone and scared. Hector, getting deeper into waters that could get them all killed. Reuben, brokenhearted that his belief in his brother had been an illusion. Anger, pride, judgment, vengefulness. All of those sins had spread their tentacles across two families who teetered on the verge of destruction. At least Mia and Gracie were safe for the moment. But what kind of life were they living? On the run with no family to support them.

Pain knifed through her as Silvio arranged the cushions on the floor in the corner of the cramped space. "Will have to do."

Rain pelted against the roof. "Is this shelter going to stand through the hurricane, Silvio?"

"She'll stand against the wind." He rapped a hand against the solid walls. "But…"

Antonia waited. "What else are you worried about?"

"We've weathered plenty of storms here in Florida, Antonia, and you know the wind is the part you can hunker down from. Get low, keep the windows closed, you'll probably survive that part."

Her mind went to a fact her heart must have kept stuffed in her subconscious. "But not the water."

"When Charley hit, we got twelve-foot waves."

Antonia looked again at the roof only a couple of feet from her head, imagining the ocean swelling to monstrous proportions.

Silvio seemed lost in thought as he, too, stared at the beams over their heads. "Tiny little island in a great big storm."

She thought about Reuben at the top of the cupola staring out at the view she now imagined, his heart heavy, his spirit low.

Tiny island.

Great big storm.

Reuben paused at the door that would lead up to the short flight of steps to the cupola. He put a hand on the solid wood and felt it tremble, as if there were a beast clawing at the other side. The walls around him rattled, and vibrations rippled through the soles of his boots. The beast had gotten in at last; Hurricane Tony had arrived.

He turned and pressed his back there, sinking to a crouching position and letting the anger of the storm hammer against his shoulders. The worst thing he could do would be to open that door and let the eighty-mile-per-hour winds into Isla to wreck and destroy anything that remained of his family.

And was there anything left of the Sandovals to save? The percussion on his back reminded him of his father's conga drum, staved sides, taut head that could be coaxed to produce so many incredible sounds with just his father's fingers and palms. In the simple days, the time before they'd moved to the big house on the beach and began to collect the speedboats, the Aston Martins, the luxury condos, his mother had danced barefoot to the beat of that conga drum, whirling her two little boys in her arms until they collapsed in a dizzy pile. Reuben's hand clenched into a fist as he added his own beating to the force hammering on the door, anger roiling through him like savage music.

He had not saved his brother.

All his prayers and effort, the conflict and confrontation, wasted in a naive belief.

And the most horrific cost of his error? He'd lost Antonia.

Bile rose in his throat.

The life they could have had, the love they could have nourished and tended over the years like his precious orange grove. Gone. Hector's crimes had overwhelmed it all. Still, maybe there was a piece he didn't see, some explanation that would excuse Hector's partnership with Leland, a way it could all be explained.

"Stop it, Reuben," he growled to no one. "Stop deluding yourself about your brother. Antonia is right. He's crooked like our father." Saying the words aloud drove them deeper into his gut.

Like our father.

His mother would have said, "God the Father is perfect, Reuben."

He knew it was true, but the knowledge did not ease the razor-sharp pain that knifed inside him.

He thought about the people huddled under his roof one story down. Gavin, Paula, Silvio, Antonia. "Father God, I cannot understand why You did not help me save my brother." He wanted to shout it, to hammer against the wooden walls loud enough for God to hear. Instead the words came out in a broken whisper. "I don't understand, but I will not turn away like my brother and my father. I will not turn away from You." He pressed his forehead to the damp door. "Help me keep them alive."

He could not force himself to say one more prayer for his brother, not one more plea to add to the discourse he'd composed over the years, not a single additional request for intercession. Instead he pressed his hand to the door and offered up only one broken word to the Father who he knew had caught every tear and anguished hope. "Hector."

He opened his eyes to find Antonia there, hair dripping diamonds onto the floor, her eyes soft.

"Reuben," she said. "I wish I had been wrong."

He stood and cleared his throat, wondering how long she had been in the stairwell. "Wishing doesn't change anything, does it?"

"No, but I was wrong to want him to fall."

Her lips trembled slightly and so did his resolve. He wanted nothing more than to bury his face in her hair, to hold close the comfort of her lips and insert himself into the circle of her embrace.

Instead he managed to edge by her, careful not to breathe in the scent of her, which he knew might break through his weakened self-control. "Is the storm shelter ready?"

"As best as we could. It's pretty jammed in there."

The lobby was dark and quiet, except for the annoyed comments from Silvio, who stood next to an open closet, receiving a pile of neatly folded blankets from Paula.

"We have enough already," Silvio grumbled. "The storm shelter is only so big, you know."

Paula answered him by plopping several more blankets into his outstretched arms. "We don't know how long we'll be in there."

They all stopped as an onslaught of wind rattled the walls.

"Did you…?" Reuben said to Silvio.

"All windows are boarded up. Back door is bolted, but we can get out if necessary. Front door is locked."

"That's never been a very solid lock," Reuben said. "I'm going to board it up."

Silvio shoved the pile of blankets into Antonia's arms. "I'm helping Reuben. You hold on to these."

Reuben grabbed the hammer from the kitchen and went to a stack of plywood he'd piled in the entry for easy access.

With Silvio on one end of the board and Reuben on the other, they levered the wood into place. He'd just placed the nail, ready to hammer, when something snapped. Reuben watched in horror as the upper hinge of the door distended and twisted, fingers of metal springing loose as it failed.

"Hold it," Reuben shouted, throwing his weight against the door and trying to get a nail steadied against the shuddering wood.

Silvio pressed his back there, his legs straining. "Hammer it down, quick," he groaned.

Reuben saw Antonia drop the blankets and start toward them.

"No," he shouted.

She made it two more steps before both the hinges gave way completely and the bolt snapped. The door blew inward, bringing the wrath of the hurricane with it.

TWELVE

Antonia was knocked backward from the impact of the wind that rushed into the hotel with the force of a runaway locomotive. Through the tangle of hair that plastered her face, she saw Reuben and Silvio fall under the heavy plywood before her view was obscured by a maelstrom of flying papers, books, cushions and whatever else the storm could liberate from shelves and bookcases.

Paula shrieked and scrambled toward Silvio but tripped and went down on the fallen pile of blankets Antonia had dropped moments before. Crawling on hands and knees, Antonia clawed her way to the front door.

Reuben was also on hands and knees, reaching under the vibrating boards to free Silvio, who emerged dazed, white hair standing on end. Silvio's eyes widened as he saw Paula on the floor, and he headed to her.

"Get to the shelter," Reuben yelled, rain thundering by him in piercing waves.

Paula scrambled to her feet and helped Silvio hoist the unconscious Gavin over his shoulder.

Reuben turned again to the plywood, trying to force it back upright against the doorjamb. His muscles bulged under the strain.

"Leave it," Antonia shouted. "You can't fix it now."

Reuben ignored her and kept up his battle with the sodden wood.

She grabbed his shoulder, muscles knotted tight under her fingers. "Stop."

His eyes burned. "I can save it."

"No, you can't," she said, pulling on him as hard as she dared.

He whirled to face her, mouth taut with anger.

They stood there, barely maintaining their footing, eyes locked on each other, and she understood so much in that moment, even though the only sound was the shriek of the storm.

I couldn't save my brother.

Isla is all that's left.

I can't lose that, too.

She wished it were not true, but the groaning of the building all around them told her he would not succeed on his quest to save Isla, like he had failed with Hector. She pressed his wrist. "You have to come to the shelter."

Silvio was already hauling Gavin toward the

kitchen. "Where's my shotgun?" he hollered. "Anyone see it?"

It would be impossible to find in the swirling wreck.

Paula stopped to scoop up Charley, who had emerged from under the sofa. They both looked at Reuben.

"They won't leave without you," Antonia said. "And neither will I."

The anger in Reuben's face drained away. He left the plywood to the wind and followed Antonia, Silvio and Paula. He stopped for only a moment, retrieving something from the floor that she could not see and stowing the item in his pocket.

It seemed as though the storm were a live thing; having gained entry, it was now pillaging Isla. When Antonia unfastened the bolt on the kitchen door, it was wrenched out of her hand, slamming open to admit the storm afresh, which began to whoosh through the space, flinging open the cupboard doors, knocking down the chairs and pulling the dishes from the shelves. Crockery crashed to the floor, flinging splinters of glass across the tile, eliciting a wail from Paula.

"Go, go," Reuben yelled, pushing Paula through after Silvio and pressing his hand on the small of Antonia's back.

She meant to move, to follow the struggling Silvio and Paula out the door, but an eerie, sucking vortex of noise stopped her. The sound was incomprehensible, unlike anything her ears had encountered before.

As if in slow motion, Reuben tilted his face upward and she did the same.

The roof.

Hurricane Tony was prying the roof off the old hotel.

So great was the shock that her brain was unable to command her body. It was Reuben who snapped to reality first and shoved her through the door. Into a crush of rain, feet sliding, eyes blinded, ears tortured by the wood tearing loose behind her, she stumbled on. Somehow she found herself at the shelter, plowing in behind Paula and Silvio, Reuben pausing as he reached for the door. She turned, too, all of them did, mesmerized by the sight before them.

It was as if the old hotel were merely a dollhouse, a child's toy, as the roof peeled away in two sections, flung loose into the wind and hurtling away toward the beach. Fragments of wood and tile eddied in dizzying circles, crashing against the remaining walls and peppering the outside of the shelter. The hurricane ripped the shutters from the walls, lifted furniture and curtains, tearing them out and casting them to the skies. Only the sturdy shelter wall behind them gave them enough protection to remain on their feet.

Antonia struggled to breathe. She had recently experienced a massive earthquake, but it was a covert killer, unleashing destruction quickly and then retreating, invisible, invincible. This force was unbridled, unhurried, lazily dismantling the island before their eyes, a horrible spectacle of brutal power.

They watched in morbid fascination as the black sky, which should have been golden with the morning sun, sucked up the spoils and whirled them out to sea.

When a piece of tile hurtled into the shelter, Reuben seemed to snap out of his reverie.

He closed the door and secured it.

No one spoke for a moment.

After a long pause, Reuben went to Silvio and helped him lay Gavin on the makeshift bed. Paula stroked the sodden cat, who mewled piteously until she put it down.

Antonia could not believe what she'd seen. Isla, the grand lady of the island, had just been torn to pieces before her eyes. She knew she would never forget the look on Reuben's face as he watched his mother's dream, his dream, splinter into pieces.

Gavin groaned and Paula went to tend to him. Reuben sat on an upended crate, elbows on his knees, while the cat curled in a crescent of wet fur around his feet. He stroked him with calloused fingers, finding the soft fur behind the cat's ears. "It's okay, Charley. It's okay."

Antonia stood frozen. She had no comfort to offer Reuben, not the faint hope that some of the hotel might survive, no reason to believe that Hector would outlast the storm or Leland. For that matter, she was not sure they would, either.

The day passed in a blur for Reuben. He was trapped in a dream, a nightmare, and somehow everyone he loved had been trapped right along with him. He watched Paula and Antonia keep busy with stacking and reorganizing the food and supplies. Paula offered sandwiches she'd made earlier, but no one would eat, much to her dismay. Silvio sat on the floor, arms crossed, a bruise darkening his cheekbone, fiddling with a battery-powered radio. He finally got a news station to come in clearly enough for them to listen to the dire facts.

Tony was now officially a Category 3 hurricane. Winds were topping eighty miles per hour as the storm battered the coast. On the mainland, power lines were down, streets flooded and rescue workers battled the elements to get to stranded victims. "The storm surge could reach as high as ten feet," the reporter said.

Ten feet.

Low pressure raised the sea level, heightening the surge. Added to that, the wave action and the natural effect of massive water volume funneling in over the gently sloping shores, through the constricting lagoon, would only increase its terrible power.

A ten-foot wall of water sweeping across Isla would inundate the storm shelter. They would have no choice but to seek shelter on the bluff where the crumbling Anchor lay. It was the only place they might survive. Might. It would also bring them out into crushing winds and within the grasp of Leland and his men, if they had managed to find shelter somewhere.

He exchanged a look with Silvio, who snapped off the radio. The way Antonia was suddenly intensely engaged in stacking soup cans told him she understood, too. They were in trouble. He wished he could pace, but there was simply no room in the shelter, crammed as it was.

He checked his phone for a message from his brother, which he knew would not come. He sent a text anyway.

Hotel gone.

He wanted to add "Where are you?" or "What have you done, Hector?" but he could not bring his fingers to push through the raw hurt bubbling in his stomach.

Gavin groaned. Paula went to him. "He's awake," she said.

They gathered around him. Gavin's eyes were

unfocused at first, until he blinked and tried to jerk upright.

Paula held him down. "Not so fast, Mr. Campbell. You've been shot, remember?"

Reuben saw Gavin put the pieces of memory together. "Where are we?"

"In the storm shelter. We found you and brought you back," Reuben said.

Gavin put a hand to his shoulder, grimacing. "Hector?"

"Gone." Reuben forced himself to ask. "Why did you come to Isla? Were you investigating my brother?"

Gavin flashed a shadow of a smile. "What? You don't like my landscaping?"

Reuben would have laughed if he weren't so close to losing it. "We know you're a cop. You were taping my brother talking to Leland."

He nodded, pain lining his forehead. "Yeah. We've been interested in Hector since he began meeting with Garza's men about nine months back."

"Nine months?" Silvio's eyes rolled in thought. "That's about when things fell apart with Mia."

Antonia's cheeks flushed. "She was right to run."

Reuben ignored the remark. Gavin was the only one who knew the truth, and he had to keep him talking. "So you came to work for me."

Gavin sucked in a breath. "Figured a good way

to keep tabs on him was by setting up a presence with you. Two birds with one stone, so to speak."

The implication was clear. "I'm not involved with Garza," Reuben spat.

Gavin shrugged. "These things tend to run in families, and your brother is in it up to his neck. He's crafty, I'll give him that much. I think he put sleeping pills in the coffee to knock us all out so there would be no resistance." He smiled. "Good thing I'm not a coffee drinker."

Silvio snorted. "Could have warned us. Some cop. Ain't you supposed to look out for people?"

He hunched painfully. "I was going to dump out the coffee, but I didn't have a chance. I had to follow Hector."

Reuben rubbed his eyes. "What do you have on my brother besides suspicions?"

Gavin laughed, then winced. "What kind of cop would I be if I told you that?" He grew serious. "Look, Reuben. Between you and me, I think you're a good guy, so I'm going to tell you that your brother cooked up some kind of deal with Garza, something having to do with Isla."

"Figures," Reuben said, swallowing a wave of bitterness.

Gavin tried to sit up again, but pain forced him back onto the cushions. "I don't know the details. I was taping when Leland heard me. I dropped my pack and took off, but not fast enough." He groaned and Paula put a hand to his brow.

"He feels hot. I'm afraid of an infection."

"Of course," Gavin said weakly. "That's the way my life has been going lately."

"Antonia," Paula ordered, "get me the antiseptic from the first-aid kit. I'll clean his wound again."

Another groan.

"Gavin." Reuben's throat went tight. "Who shot you?"

Gavin's eyes grew unfocused with the pain and closed. Antonia held the antiseptic bottle while Paula carefully peeled off the bandage, stained with fresh blood.

"Probably hurt him carrying him over," Paula clucked.

"He'd have hurt himself more crawling over on his own," Silvio grunted.

Reuben put his face close to Gavin's. "I have to know what happened."

Paula tried to push him away. "Not now, Reuben."

She was right, but he could not stop the question. Laying a hand on Gavin's arm, he pressed close. "Gavin, did Leland shoot you, or my brother?"

Gavin's eyes opened and closed again.

"Gav, tell me. Who shot you?"

"Don't know," Gavin murmured. "Could've been Leland or Hector. Hard to tell with the storm."

Reuben sat back with a sigh, and Paula edged him out of the way.

"Hector thinks he's in control," Gavin whispered. "He's wrong."

"Wrong about what?" Reuben said. "What is going on? What is Hector trying to accomplish?"

"Is he trying to get Isla for himself?" Antonia ventured. "To get back into the business and Garza isn't happy about it?"

"No…" Reuben broke off. He was going to say that Hector was trying to help him save Isla.

But was it the truth?

He did not know anymore. Like the storm was transforming the island, so was his belief in his brother, now changed and morphed into something he no longer held on to with that unshakable faith.

Whatever the details, Hector had made his choice, and now they would all have to try and survive it.

THIRTEEN

Antonia thought she might possibly go mad. Outside the shelter shook with the continued onslaught of the storm. Had it lessened? Were the winds gentling ever so slightly, or was that wishful thinking?

She'd helped Paula warm up soup on the camp stove and distributed it in paper cups, which Silvio drank straight off. She and Reuben managed a few swallows to appease Paula, and Gavin did not regain consciousness long enough to take any of it.

The hours wore on. Sometimes Silvio would turn on the radio and they would listen to the devastation played out in report after report until he silenced it. Paula spread out blankets on the floor in the corner opposite Gavin, and she and Antonia laid down to rest. Charley the cat curled up next to Gavin.

Reuben and Silvio sat on boxes in silence. When Reuben thought she wasn't watching he would cast a wary glance at the door.

Waiting for Leland?

Or the flood of water?

She thought about the most recent picture she had of Gracie, taken before Mia ran away with her. Scrawled on the back was the caption New Choppers!

Picturing little Gracie sporting shiny new teeth made Antonia smile. She wanted to tell Reuben about it, but she feared it might add salt to his stinging wounds. Looking at his profile in the dark, slumped shoulders, head down, she had the urge to go to him, to comfort, to put her cheek next to his and mingle their strength together.

She took a slow breath. Gracie was the important one now, keeping her safe, far away from Hector. Survive the storm and Leland and get away.

She did not know if Mia was even still in the state of Florida. Maybe Antonia would go join her and they'd start again in a totally new place. Her imagination took her to the mountains, a small country town.

Away from her beloved ocean that offered up vistas so breathtaking she could never capture it fully in her paintings. And away from Reuben. Finally, with Hector out of their lives, her estrangement from Reuben would be complete. A pang of grief licked at her insides.

It hurt. It would always hurt.

God help me to be strong for Gracie and Mia.

Who would be left behind to be strong for Reuben?

She closed her eyes to shut out his pensive shadow and slept.

When she awoke two hours later, the interior of the shelter was humid and stuffy, and the wind still beat angry fists against the outside walls. Paula slept next to her, wrapped so tightly in the blanket that only her face showed. Silvio sat cross-legged, back against the wall, snoring.

She sat up and blinked the confusion away. Reuben was still perched on the wooden box, the radio held up to his ear, volume turned down low. Carefully extricating herself from the blankets, she went to him.

He jerked in surprise, standing immediately to offer her his seat on the crate.

Typical Reuben. Gentleman farmer. She waved a hand. "No, thanks," she whispered. "I'll just pull up a cushion."

He sat again. "Did you sleep?"

"Some. Not you?"

He shook his head. "Silvio needs the sleep more than I do."

They listened for a moment to the chatter of the storm.

"I think the eye is approaching."

She let out a breath. "Smooth sailing ahead?"

He sighed. "You and I both know the worst of the storm comes after the eye passes."

"Can we get out of here? Move to higher ground?"

He didn't answer, and the silence stirred her anxiety.

"Leland's guys…and Hector…will be free to move then, too," she guessed. "If they survived part one of the storm. That's what you're worried about."

"I'm worried about everyone surviving this thing, that's all." He looked around. "None of this should have happened. No one should be here on Isla to face this but me." His gaze locked on hers. "Look, Nee." He scrubbed a hand across his face. "I'm sorry. I'm sorry my family problems bled over into your life and Mia's. I've been blind, just like you said, and I truly regret that I led us to this, that you ever became involved with the Sandovals."

Her lungs squeezed and she moved closer, taking his hand. "I'm not sorry."

He cocked his head. "What?"

"I'm not sorry I met you, Reuben. We had some amazing times together, and yes, it ended in a big mess, but at least we can hang on to those good memories, right? Sweet and bitter, just like oranges. Isn't that what you used to say?"

His eyes glimmered softly, the curve of his mouth reminding her of the tender kisses and gentlest of words. "I don't know why, but I was thinking of Yeats, from my mother's old poetry books." He stroked a tentative finger along her cheek. "'But one man loved the pilgrim soul in you and loved the sorrows of your changing face.'"

She closed her eyes against the tenderness spiraling through her nerves.

"I loved you more because of our trouble, not in spite of it," he whispered. "I hope you can remember some of those good times someday."

Warmth spread through her body, anchored in that touch. "Yes, I will always remember."

She felt his lips on her forehead, grazing along her eyebrows and moving to her cheekbones.

"Will you tell Gracie someday?" he said into her ear. "Tell her that Uncle Booben was a good guy way back when?"

"You never stopped being a good guy," she whispered, finally daring to open her eyes. "Things just got in the way."

"I let them get in the way. I see the shadows there in your eyes." He slid a finger under her chin and lifted her face, bending until his mouth was inches from hers. "Love isn't enough sometimes, is it?" he said, gazing into her eyes. "It wasn't enough to save my brother, and it wasn't enough to save us. This storm's just too big."

He leaned closer, and she thought for one electric moment that he meant to kiss her, but instead he pressed his mouth to her ear. "Go back to sleep, Nee. Things will look better in the morning."

Heart pounding, an ache spreading through her body, she returned to the blanket and closed her eyes.

She did finally fall asleep, waking again long before sunup. An unpleasant dampness wormed its way into her subconscious until she snapped awake, wind whirling by her face and then dying away. She sat up, wiping rain from her cheeks, hearing Silvio's angry muttering. Her watch read 3:00 a.m.

"What is it?" she called to Silvio.

"Foolishness, that's what," he grumbled.

Paula got to her feet. "Where's Reuben?"

Antonia's stomach knotted. The wind on her face, the rain spattered blankets. Someone had opened the door. She groaned. "He went after Hector."

Silvio didn't bother to affirm her conclusion. "He got a text from Hector. Said he's holing up at the Anchor and everything's a big misunderstanding. Asked him to come."

Antonia felt her breath catch. "It's a trap. Hector's lying."

"Probably," Silvio said, "but Reuben thinks it's the only way to put an end to it and keep us all safe."

"He can't do that," Antonia said, throat thick with fear.

"He already did. Eye of the storm is here, so we've got about an hour, I figure, before the storm hammers us again. I've got to check the water level. You stay here and help Paula care for Gavin."

"I'm going after Reuben," Antonia said, heading for the door.

Silvio grabbed her arm. "No. If the flood comes, I'll need your help to get Paula and Gavin out. I can't do it myself."

Her mind reeled. "But Reuben…"

Silvio shook his head gently. "He doesn't want you to go after him." He handed her a paper-wrapped lump. "He told me to give you this."

She looked from the paper to Silvio. He patted her shoulder. "I'll be back as soon as I can. Stay here and help Paula. Don't open the door unless you know it's me." He left, and Paula slid the bolt behind him.

Antonia sat down on the blankets, clutching the little bundle. What had Reuben gone to do? He would sacrifice himself to save them, to save her, after she had done everything to wound him with the truth about Hector.

Tears stung her eyes. With fingers gone cold, she unwrapped the lump. It was the junonia shell, now chipped even more than it had been, but still intact. She pressed the glassy surface to her cheek, the coolness against her hot skin comforting. On the paper was a short note in Reuben's strange handwriting, all capital letters.

Nee,
Hope you can still see the beauty in this. I'm
sorry.
Reuben

Crumpling the paper and pressing it to her heart,
she began to cry.

Reuben took the steps to the Anchor slowly, wad-
ing around enormous puddles as best he could. He
stopped at the top of the hill littered with downed
trees and broken branches and looked to the distance, where the Isla Hotel had once stood. Moonlight still filtered between the clouds and painted
the island with eerie hues.

Only two exterior walls remained, the windows
blown out and odd bits of curtain still clinging to
protruding nails, fluttering in the breeze like flags
of surrender. Ruined beyond repair. He was probably supposed to be feeling grief, but instead he felt a
strange sense of relief. It was no longer in his power
to save the old relic. He could lay that burden down
and focus on the other one that lanced at his heart.

He intended to sign over whatever Garza wanted
if it would extricate his brother and protect Antonia
and Gracie. One last chance to save them. The land
seemed a small thing now. It was the only collateral
he had, and he would give it willingly.

Maybe it would appease Garza, or maybe he would kill Reuben anyway, but it was a risk that had to be taken. Leland and his men would no longer need to go after Antonia once they had their prize.

The water level along the shore had risen, swamping the dock where Reuben's burned boats bobbed like ugly black refuse. The *Black-Eyed Beauty*. He felt the kindle of anger. That loss hurt him more than the hotel.

He wished he had binoculars so he could climb a tree and try to catch a glimpse of the boathouse. It was a sturdy structure that had survived hurricanes before, but it was still unlikely the thugs had been able to hide out there for too long.

Leaves crackled in the trees, and though he kept as keen an eye out as he could, he saw no signs of any pursuers. Reaching the Anchor, he was astonished to see that the old lighthouse still stood. Apart from new chunks knocked loose by the wind, the structure appeared intact. He smiled. His mother would be pleased.

The smile vanished as he saw the board was removed from the opening. Hector was waiting for him at the top.

Or was it Leland?

He made sure his knife was still clipped to his belt, though he knew it would prove somewhat useless against Garza's men. Reuben was not a street fighter, but he'd do his best to defend himself and his brother. With no more time to talk himself out of it, he started up the stone steps.

The steps were wet, the walls dripping with a combination of humidity and the rain that had lashed its way in through the missing bricks. He placed each foot silently, stopping every few steps to listen. No sound, not even the wind. It was as if the hurricane had been suddenly switched off, leaving only serene calm in its wake. Only a trick, he knew. Once the eye passed, the most violent weather, the storm wall, was waiting to punish them.

Halfway up he heard a low creak. Someone walking? The old metal of the Fresnel lens buckling? Hair on the back of his neck prickled. He slid the knife from its sheath and held it before him. Fifteen more steps. He stopped to catch his breath, wondering if he should try to text Hector again but fearing the light from his phone would make him an easy target if Leland were waiting.

Moonlight filtered down from the top of the steps, and it was enough for him to step around the broken places. There was no way to avoid the bits of brick that ground under his feet, crunching loudly in the silent space. Whoever it was could hear Reuben coming, and they'd be ready.

Fine. If it's Leland, let's make him earn his pay.

Knife ready, Reuben took a deep breath and sprinted up the last ten steps, hurtling into the dark nest at the top of the Anchor. The lens sparkled with glints of moonlight, and a wisp of cigarette smoke drifted across the glass.

"Hector?" Reuben said.

His brother stepped from behind the massive structure, cigarette held in his shaking hand.

Reuben took an involuntary step forward. Hector had received a beating, it was clear. His left eye was nearly swollen shut, jacket torn and rumpled, smears of dark on what had once been an expensive silk shirt. "What happened?"

Hector did not look at him, instead gazing out at the eerily calm panorama below. "I want you to know I was out of it all."

"The business?"

"Yes. Just like you begged me to do, prayed and all that, I know. I was out. I was making a life with Mia and Gracie. I did not let you down."

"What happened, Hector?" Reuben said, trying to press away the anguish he somehow knew was going to come next.

"He came to me. Leland, Garza's man. He told me my services would be needed to get you to hand over Isla."

"What kind of services?"

Hector blew out a long stream of smoke. "Point is, I was doing it, staying clean, trying to take the high road, and they showed me I couldn't stay out."

"Why not?" He readied himself for another of

his brother's excuses, sliding the knife back into its sheath.

Hector looked at him. "They have pictures of me, from the last drug deal I was a part of. You don't cooperate, they told me, and the pictures go to the police. I go to jail and never see my daughter again."

Reuben let out a huge breath. "Oh, no."

Hector turned his gaze back to the sea. "I know Mia and I are over. We shouldn't have gotten together in the first place, and I scared her badly, which is why she stabbed me. She never meant to hurt me, but she was trying to protect Gracie. Gracie is the best thing I ever did, the only good thing I ever produced, probably. I couldn't stand the idea of never seeing her again, of her growing up knowing her father was in prison."

Something cold gathered in the pit of Reuben's stomach. "What did you agree to do for them?"

"Get you to hand over Isla."

"Your job was to persuade me to do that?"

He nodded. "I came up with a plan, a surefire way to do that so no one would get killed. They were prepared to kill you and go after Gracie and Mia to get me to sign after your death, but I figured out a way." He began to pace. "You see, I figured out a way where no one would get hurt."

"What way?" he forced himself to ask.

"It would have worked, but Leland changed everything. I tried to stop it, thought I could drug the coffee and while you were all sleeping talk to Leland and convince him the plan would still work. He wouldn't listen, of course. He found out there is a cop on the island, and he was going to finish the job before things got any worse."

"Hector," Reuben said, voice low and level. "Tell me what your deal was with Garza."

His brother's eyes flicked to the floor. "I arranged for Antonia to be kidnapped."

"What?" The words exploded from his mouth.

"Leland was supposed to snatch her from the beach." He shook his head impatiently. "I know you still love her and you'd never let them hurt her. They would just hold her for a while, you'd sign over the island and then they'd let her go, no harm done."

"No harm done?" he bellowed. "You were going to deliver her to a bunch of criminals? And you were dumb enough to think they'd let her go again?"

"She's too smart to ever testify against them."

Reuben grabbed Hector by the collar. "You put her in danger to save your own skin."

"And yours, brother," Hector hissed. "And besides, Antonia can take care of herself, remember? She's helping Mia keep me from my daughter."

Reuben shoved him backward, trying to control his rage. "You don't deserve Gracie. She doesn't need a father like that."

Hector's eyes sparked. "She's my daughter. I'll have her back."

"Really? Now that you've made a deal with Garza's men that's gone wrong? What makes you think they aren't going to turn you over to the police to get even?"

"We didn't foresee Antonia making it to Isla, but it will still work." A cloud eased across the moon and left them in a moment of darkness before it drifted to the other side.

"I will sign away the island," he hissed through gritted teeth. "Leland can have it. They can leave and it's done."

"Leland thinks in black and white. He's decided to take things into his own hands and clean up the mess. I tried to convince him there was no need to go through with it."

Reuben's heart thudded to a stop. He stared at his brother. "He's going after Antonia anyway, in spite of the cops? And the storm? And whatever you said to him? Just to make sure I sign it over?"

"He's a cautious psychopath."

"He won't be able to get to her with this hurricane…" Reuben broke off. The eye. The reprieve from the storm. A sick certainty trickled up his spine. "That's why you asked me to come meet you, isn't it?"

Hector didn't answer.

"He's going after her now, isn't he?"

Time stood still before Hector answered. "Yes."

Reuben turned on his heel and plunged back down the steps, heedless now of the deteriorating cement under his feet.

"I tried to call it off, Reuben," Hector's desperate voice floated down. "I never meant for her to get hurt."

Reuben let his brother's words die away behind him as he sprinted into the darkness.

FOURTEEN

Antonia paced the tiny floor, trying to stay out of Paula's way as she tended to Gavin, who seemed more feverish than he had hours before. She checked her watch compulsively, trying to decide if Reuben had had time to get to the Anchor for his meeting with Hector. If it even was a meeting and not an ambush by Leland.

Several times she started for the door and Paula called her back.

"Do what Silvio said," she snapped. "You'll only make things worse."

Was it possible that things could get worse? She continued her abbreviated pacing, praying fervently that God would spare Reuben's life. All the months she'd spent entreating Him to unmask Hector, to convince Reuben that his brother was a criminal. She realized she'd been asking God for the wrong thing. Judgment was God's department, mercy was supposed to be hers.

She had not been merciful, had not wanted anything better for Hector than incarceration and nothing more for Reuben than to realize he was wrong. Pain throbbed in her temples.

"When will Silvio be back?" she said.

"When he's done," Paula sniped. "He's not out on a pleasure stroll."

Antonia huffed. The minutes ticked on in painful slow motion. It was still hours from sunrise. The eye would not last much longer. Her pace increased until she bumped into Paula as she made for the first-aid kit.

"Will you sit down? This isn't..." Paula's words trailed off, eyes suddenly fixed on the door.

Antonia followed her gaze. At first she couldn't see it, but the bitter scent helped her understand.

"Smoke," Antonia shouted. "The shelter's on fire."

Paula did not waste a moment. "We'll have to carry him out," she said, taking Gavin by the shoulders and getting ready to move him. "Open the door, quickly."

Antonia grabbed the bolt and unlocked it.

The door slammed open, and at first she thought the storm wall had arrived again. Through a cloud of black smoke she felt hands grab her arms, and she was dragged out of the shelter.

She kicked and clawed at the strange pockmarked man who held her until he forced her to the ground and secured her wrists behind her back with duct tape. When he rolled her over, she saw Leland behind him, standing with the burning rag he'd shoved in the crack under the door.

"Hello, *señorita.* Ready to come out and play?"

Paula appeared in the doorway holding a small knife. "Leave her be. Get away."

Leland laughed. "Hello, Granny. You're too busy to come after me. Storm's on the way and you've got to help Gramps. He's not feeling too well. We left him down by the water."

Paula's mouth trembled in fear. The pockmarked man shoved her back inside and tossed in a lantern. The glass smashed and sent flaming kerosene showering onto the pile of bedding.

"No," Antonia shouted as the blankets caught, Paula still on her knees where she had fallen. She crawled toward the shelter. "Paula," she cried.

Through a thick curtain of fear, Antonia was pulled to her feet so quickly her head spun. "You can't leave her," she shouted again. "Let go of me." In spite of her kicking and flailing, she could not fight her way through the two men back to the shelter.

"Sorry, my girl," Leland said. "We've got an appointment and we must be off before the eye gives way."

"Where are you taking me?" she gasped, still trying to squirm out of their grip and reach Paula and Gavin.

"Back to the mainland," Leland said. "We've got

just enough time to make it, I'd say. Lost one of our boats, but we really need only one anyway."

"What are you going to do with me there?"

Leland ignored her, walking briskly along the path, skirting the flooded portions as best he could.

"I said what are you going to do with me?" she hollered, fear turning momentarily to anger.

He didn't turn. The other man pushed her forward with a shove to the shoulder blades. They took the path that sloped down to the lagoon. The water level was now several feet higher than it had been, but the skimmer was unscathed, bobbing gracefully in the small pocket of lagoon, shielded by the palm tree to which it was tied.

Leland stopped at the edge of the water. "Go, Martin. Untie the skimmer and bring it as close to shore as you can."

Once they got her on that boat, she knew her fate would be sealed. "Is this part of the deal you made with Hector? Hand me over to Garza and force Reuben to give you Isla?"

Leland still did not look her way. "Look at all that water," he said. "Incredible."

She edged back a step. "I guess that means you work for Hector."

Leland laughed. "Hector is soft. He made us promise not to hurt you as if we're kids on the playground at recess." He called to Martin. "We're in a rush, remember."

She took the moment to bolt. Up the path she churned, legs slipping, but not losing her balance. Pulse throbbing, she ran as fast as she dared, awkward with her hands secured behind her back. She'd make it to the Anchor, to Reuben, or far enough away to find a hiding place.

She knew she was not alone on the path. From behind her came the sound of feet moving quickly. She had only a few precious moments to make her escape.

As he cleared the door and emerged into the storm-washed air, Hector grabbed Reuben from behind and spun him around.

"You have to believe me, Reuben. I did not mean for her to get hurt."

"I don't have time to listen to your excuses."

"I did it to try to save you…." His eyes were pleading.

Reuben felt a horrible calm come over him. He stepped back. "No, you did it to save yourself. You wanted to be a father to Gracie, to have all the good parts of what it means to have a family. Well, you know what? Having a family means doing the hard thing, taking responsibility and being a man. I tried to help you see that, but I'm not enough."

"No," Hector began.

"I'm not enough," Reuben shouted. "I can't save

you, and I shouldn't have tried. That's between you and God."

"Don't go after her," Hector said, voice hoarse. "Let them do their thing. You'll get her back. I promise."

Reuben shook his head. "Your promises mean nothing to me, not anymore."

He turned and stopped short. A stain appeared against the sky, a dark inky splotch outlined against the silver sky. It was a cloud of smoke. Now he thought he could detect the acrid tang of something burning there, over the swell of ground where the shelter should be. He allowed one glance at Hector, and he saw the shock in his brother's eyes, the realization that he had put his fate in the hands of evil men.

With his brother's stricken look burned into his heart, Reuben sprinted away from the Anchor. He made good time in spite of the clinging mud, until he got to the small bridge that spanned what had been the modest creek. The storm had dumped so much water into the creek that it had overflowed the channel and submerged the bridge, eating up the banks on either side until the water thundered along. He did not dare risk trying to swim across. The span was only twelve feet or so, but the water crashed by so violently he knew he would be swept away.

Reversing course, he backed up to higher ground and made his own way through the ferns in the direction of the shelter. With each step, his gut clenched, nerves firing.

Paula. Silvio. Gavin. Antonia. He knew his pride had blinded him to the truth and put four people in harm's way.

I can save them, I can save them, his mind chanted.

Like you saved Hector?

He pressed on, splashing through a puddle that had grown to lake size, the water reaching his shins, until he saw the wrecked Isla Hotel at the top of the next ridge. Not sparing a glance he charged up, past the ruined structure and on until he came to a dead stop.

Heart thundering, he looked in horror at the storm shelter, which was fully engulfed in flames, yellow tongues of fire licking at the flat roof. Tearing along the path he arrived in time to see the lintel giving way, cracking into two splintered fragments in the open door.

He started shouting words that were probably incoherent as he sheltered his face against the smoke and heat and tried to make entry. A figure moved in the shadows and he yelled again, kicking at the broken wood that blocked the door.

The wood relinquished and he grabbed at the person, yanking them both back away from the burning shelter. It was Silvio, face blackened, coughing hard.

Reuben supported him as they stumbled away,

until he let him go several yards from the shelter and turned back.

"No," Silvio grunted until a coughing fit choked off his words.

Reuben did not wait for him to recover but ran back to the shelter, which seemed to light the entire sky, given added power by the rising sun. He was knocked back a step when the shelter collapsed, beams settling in on themselves, releasing a cloud of stinging smoke.

He made it to his knees, witnessing with disbelieving eyes what his heart told him could not be true.

There was no more shelter and nothing left alive inside.

Moonlight helped Antonia pick out the trail as she fled. It looked strange since the storm had rewritten the terrain. An enormous pine sprawled across the path. Too big to climb over. No choice but to go around. Fear left her clumsy and she caught a foot in the tangle of roots, landing on the sodden ground. Breath caught, nerves firing, she scrambled to her knees when she felt him behind her. Leland yanked her up by the arm.

To her surprise, she saw he was smiling. "I told them it was too much trouble. The whole abduction thing? Idiocy." He laughed. "You would do something dumb, I told Mr. Garza. Attract attention, maybe require us to hurt you, and then where would we be?"

"What are you talking about?" she breathed.

"The whole abduction thing," he said. "It's not like you'd just forgive and forget if we let you go after Reuben capitulated. You don't forgive. You're not that kind."

She could not understand. He was not speaking sense.

"I don't bother with forgiveness, either." He laughed. "Cut off the hand that hurt you and you don't have to bother with the whole forgiveness thing."

"You're insane."

He did not seem to hear, calling to Martin. "I'm changing the plan. Two for the mainland," he said cheerfully as he pushed her toward the edge of the lagoon. "Watch out for alligators. I hate those things," he said, peering into the lapping water.

Two for the mainland? She felt the cold chill of terror, heard the soft ring of a knife being removed from the sheath. The skin on her neck prickled as he leaned close, and she tensed for the blade to be plunged into her back. Cold sweat beaded on her forehead. When he came close, maybe there would be a moment, one more second, one last chance.

Instead, there was a ripping sound and she realized he was cutting the tape that bound her wrists.

Disbelief pounded through her. She pulled her

hands free and ripped off the tape. "You're letting me go?"

He laughed again. "Yes, you are free to escape as long as you head that way." He took out a gun and pointed toward the swollen sea.

She stared. "What?"

"Swim, little Antonia," he said, fluttering the fingers of his free hand. "Swim away into the ocean, like a lovely mermaid heading for Atlantis."

Reality hit home with a sickening thud. He was going to watch her drown. "Reuben will never give you Isla if you kill me."

"I'm not going to kill you. You're going to be offed by this terrible hurricane," he said. "And so is Reuben, now that I think on it. The shelter is destroyed and he's got no place to hunker down to ride out this storm. The abduction thing is ridiculous, and I told Mr. Garza as much, but he's old and he doesn't stomach murder very well anymore, especially the murder of women. Soft."

Her stomach heaved. *Keep him talking.* Anything to delay her entry into that idling ocean. "And Hector? What about him?"

"You see? You've got the critical piece. Hector is really all we need after you and Reuben are dead. He'll sign over Isla. I told Mr. Garza that, too." He shook his head in disgust.

"Maybe he won't."

Leland settled on a seat in the skimmer after

Martin untied the boat. "Sure he will. Hector's a coward, through and through, but he loves his kid and we've got photos that can put him away. That's why he arranged this idiot kidnapping idea."

Bile rose in her throat. He'd done it for Gracie, thinking he could control this madman. What a colossal miscalculation.

"And now that he's shot a cop, he's got no wiggle room."

"So he shot Gavin?"

"He was aiming for me." Leland chuckled. "Storm conditions threw him off." Leland pulled a gun from his waistband. "Off you go. Into the water now."

"Does Mr. Garza know he's got a monster working for him?"

Leland smiled. "I'm not a monster. Monsters care. I don't." He pointed again with the gun. "Get swimming."

"No." She forced the words out. "You'll have to shoot me and the cops will know it was murder."

He sighed. "If I must, I must. But I'll just wound you a little and let the alligators take care of the rest." He jerked. "Look. There's one slithering into the water right now. Hurricanes don't throw off an alligator's need to feed. They're like killing machines."

She was not sure if there really was an alligator circling the lagoon or if it was another sick game. Shivering, she moved into the water, shin deep. Stall for time. The storm wall was approaching and

Leland would have to leave within minutes. As soon as he did she might be able to make it back to the lagoon. Somehow. She'd find Reuben. She'd find him.

The water lapped at her knees as she moved past the juncture where the lagoon would intermingle with the ocean. She could feel the currents pulling and tugging at her legs, and soon she had to tread water.

The skimmer edged along behind.

"Faster, little mermaid," Leland sang out.

With one more look behind at Isla and one more anguished thought of Reuben and his friends, she struck out for the ocean.

FIFTEEN

Reuben did not feel the flames licking at his shirt. He could not feel anything but anguish ripping through him, white hot and spreading. Then Silvio was there, knocking him down, rolling him over into the wet ground and smothering his smoldering shirtsleeve.

Silvio hauled him to his feet. Reuben breathed hard, tearing away the sleeve that was hot to the touch, the smell of singed flesh assaulting his nostrils.

Silvio was still coughing so hard he could not speak, so he settled for a gesture, jabbing his finger toward a pile of debris caught by the palms some fifteen feet away from the shelter. Something moved there; someone peeked from behind the pile. He wiped his stinging eyes and looked again. It was Paula, face terribly white.

Reuben ran, Silvio staggering after.

Rounding the wall of ruins, he found Paula tucked beneath a dripping screen of shrubs, tears running down her face, and Gavin sitting upright propped against a broken board. As Paula embraced him, he felt her shuddering sobs. He held her close, thanking God that she was unharmed, until his senses began to function again.

"Antonia?" he gasped.

Paula gripped his arms. "She wasn't inside."

The relief left him dizzy for a moment. She was alive. Antonia was alive.

Gavin shook his head. "Your brother runs with a mean crowd. Leland left us there to burn to death. Paula tried to smother the flames, but they were too much. We half crawled, half walked out of that trap only by the grace of God."

Reuben looked at Silvio. "And what happened to you?"

"Leland and his guy found me at the shore and came after me, but I'm quick for an old-timer and I know this island better than any man alive. Hid out in the mangroves till they got tired of waiting."

Paula gave him a withering look. "And then my hero had to go back in to the shelter again even though I begged him not to."

"Not once, but twice," Gavin added.

Reuben ogled. "What in the world did you do that for?"

Silvio glared at them. "In case you ain't noticed, we're about to get slammed by Hurricane Tony part two, and now we got no shelter." He unloaded a package of bread and a bottle of water. "I figured we at least got to have something to eat and those couple of blankets I saved, if we're going to stay alive."

Reuben let out a breath. "You're right. Practical to the end. So Leland's gone. Where's Antonia?" He watched their faces grow dead serious in the space of a second. Paula looked at her husband. "Where is she?" he repeated.

"Son—" Silvio started, then broke off.

Reuben tried to catch his eyes, but Silvio looked at his feet.

"Somebody tell me what's going on right now," he said, nerves whip taut.

"Leland took her," Gavin said softly. "Just before he set the fire."

Reuben's heart stuttered to a stop. "Where?"

"I didn't see," Paula said. "I tried to get to her, but the fire…"

Silvio put an arm on her narrow shoulders. "You couldn't have done anything 'bout it."

"I got one look before the place caught," Gavin said. "He headed toward the lagoon." He added quietly, "They bound her hands."

Bound her hands. He closed his eyes against the image, trying to piece together what he should do. Swallowing hard, he looked at them. "Get to the Anchor. It's the only place that might withstand the storm wall. Hector was there a while ago, but it's our only choice now. I'm going to get Antonia."

Gavin hauled himself to his feet. "I'm going with you."

"You can't keep up."

"I'm tougher than I look," he said with a tight smile.

"You need to stay with them. I don't know where Leland is and exactly how many guys he's got."

Gavin's eyes narrowed. "And your brother? Which side is he on exactly? Yours or Leland's?"

Reuben took a deep breath. "He's on his own side, always has been. Get to the Anchor and close it up. We don't have much time now."

Even as he took off, the moist air rippling through his burned shirt, he could see the storm eating up the sunrise, the columns of angry clouds gobbling the horizon. Hurricane Tony was ready again for battle. Paula grasped him in another hug, and he pressed her close. She was trembling now, struggling to contain the emotion, determined to hold back her sobs.

"It will be okay," he whispered to her, leaning to kiss the top of her head. "I need you to take care of these good-for-nothing men," he added with a smile.

She sniffed and took a deep, shuddering breath. "Reuben Sandoval, don't you get yourself killed, do you hear me? Or you're in big trouble, mister, and I mean it."

He smiled. Silvio gave him a gruff nod, which he

understood to mean that he echoed his wife's sentiment. Gavin offered his good hand for a shake.

"I gotta say, for an orange grower, you're one tough dude."

Reuben shook his hand. "And for a gardener, you got some guts, too."

Gavin gripped his palm. "I'll get reinforcements here the minute I can get a call through. Take care, man. Bad folks with nothing to lose are ruthless. Remember that."

Guys with everything to lose can be ruthless, too. He left them with a silent prayer and headed to detour around the pockets of debris and the overflowing creek. As he ran, the rain started up again, just a sprinkle, the first quiet warning that things were about to change. Far away over the mainland, lightning sizzled through the blackened sky.

With the storm building around him, and the ruined hotel behind, Reuben felt the slap of truth hit home. He wanted nothing in that moment but to save Antonia. She would never be his and he would live with that pain, but she had to survive these perfect twin storms of Tony and Leland.

Scrambling across a fallen tree, he remembered a long-ago day and the three beige speckled plover's eggs lying ruined in a scattered nest on the beach, pecked apart by a hungry gull. Antonia shooed away the gull, but it was too late to save the plover's eggs. He recalled how she'd crouched there for a long while, staring at the gummy bits of broken shell, her eyes filled with tears. He'd tried to comfort her.

"They weren't chicks yet, just eggs," he'd offered clumsily.

She turned wet eyes on him, filled with some emotion that was deeper and richer than any he experienced then. "They won't ever become what they were meant to be."

It was what he felt now. Antonia was a vibrant woman, filled with compassion, love and an ability to see things that others couldn't. He loved her. He'd always love her and probably always had, and though he could not save her for himself, he would not give up trying to keep her alive until the last breath was hammered out of him.

Lord, I've been blind, and I've tried to do things my way, to save Hector by my own actions. I forgot that You are the only One who saves. Please, Lord. Please save Antonia. He could not manage any more as he slid down the hill through the rain toward the swollen lagoon.

Antonia swam only about ten yards before she felt the change in the ocean. All around her the waves began to grow restless, driven by the wind that blew out of nowhere to lash her face. The storm wall rose in the distance like a massive creature come to devour her. Looking back, she saw Leland and Martin behind her, heard them ramping up the engine. A few more yards and the ocean would suck her away. They would race the hurricane back to the mainland, hoping to be just ahead of the storm wall, and leave her there alone to die.

Something slid next to her and she nearly screamed. Alligators. Her throat closed up in fear until she saw the ungainly lines of an enormous manatee. The creature was longer than she was; the blunt, whiskered snout poked through the surface, snuffling air not six inches from her face. With long, graceful flippers the mother guided a plump baby along as they slowly meandered by on their way toward the lagoon. Antonia knew the animal was heading for the grass beds in the sheltered water where she and her baby could wait out the storm. She wished she could do the same.

Waves stung her eyes and she blinked, the air rumbling around her as the manatees departed. She tried to guess how much longer it would be before the hurricane hit full force. If she could dally, Leland might have to leave before she was properly drowned. Then again, he might lose patience and shoot her, leaving her to the alligators.

The sound of thwacking rotors electrified her. Overhead in the distance was an orange-and-white helicopter, hovering low, as if searching for something. Her heart leaped.

Gavin's report or Reuben's phone call to the authorities had worked. The coast guard chopper droned closer.

"Hey," Antonia screamed, waving her hands as much as she could while still staying afloat. "I'm here! Here!"

The helicopter was close enough now that she could make out the white stripe on the tail and a glimpse of the wheels. She waved more furiously, darting a glance behind her, and saw the skimmer reverse course, returning to the screen of the lagoon where they would not be spotted.

Never mind Leland for now. She had to get the coast guard's attention and tell them there were people trapped on the island, innocent people who desperately needed help.

She hollered again, trying to lift herself above the cresting waves.

The helicopter moved closer and she swam a few strokes, spitting out water and hollering again until her throat burned. "Here, please, please," she shouted.

For one more moment the helicopter moved closer, the shadow nearly touching Antonia where she struggled to stay afloat while still wildly waving her arms. Then it turned and headed the other direction, no doubt deciding conditions were too dangerous for the aircraft.

"No!" She slammed the water in frustration. "Don't leave us," she screamed into an ocean that swallowed up the sound. In a matter of minutes, the helicopter had disappeared from sight.

Her spirit seemed to break within her. Arms heavy, legs like lead weights, she began to sink. She did not have the strength to make it back to the lagoon, and Leland would make sure she would not receive shelter there anyway. Ahead of her, the mainland stretched an impossibly far distance away, blotted out by the advancing storm that now buffeted the water around her into a frenzy. Too far. Impossible.

There seemed no other choice but to give up and stop fighting, let herself be pulled out to the ocean without battling the inevitable. Profound fatigue soaked into every muscle fiber, every pore.

No, came the very small whisper into her mind. She grabbed hold of it and started to chastise herself. *You will not give up. You will not leave those people behind. You will not leave your sister and Gracie.*

And Reuben.

She turned on her back, face to the rain, and rested as much as she could, trying to steady her breathing against the panic that nibbled away at the edges of her mind.

You will not give up.

She chanted it over and over in her head. *Will not.* She flipped over and tried again to discern which direction would get her to shore away from Leland. A flash of lightning illuminated the water for a split second, time enough for her to realize she was about a half mile away from a long spit of land that jutted out just past the Anchor. If she could make it there, bypassing the lagoon where Leland lay waiting, she might reach shore.

This time the storm would be her advantage, she decided. The rain was pummeling down so hard it would be difficult for Leland to spot her, a tiny speck amongst so much chaos. Sucking in a deep breath she allowed herself to be driven on the waves for a while, fighting the constant deluge of salt water and rain. By her rough estimation, she should tread water every few feet and reconnoiter. There was only one chance for success. If she let the waves carry her too far, she'd be swept past the spit and there would be no chance of fighting her way back. If she tarried too long treading water, she might not have the strength to claw her way onto the land.

Fatigue was rapidly overcoming her mental reserves. Her shoulder muscles burned from the effort of keeping her afloat. It was impossible to avoid swallowing mouthfuls of seawater, and her eyes began to blur from the stinging rain. *You will not give up.*

Just a little longer, she told herself, but she realized she was barely resisting the sucking tide. Body cold, thoughts becoming fuzzy, vision blurred. A wave crashed over her head and she was pushed down. Emerging a moment later spluttering and coughing, she went under again when the next wave caught her.

Terror rippling her body, she made it to the surface again. Something bumped her shoulder. She recoiled in terror, her mind spinning with thoughts of alligators or the great white sharks, which she and Reuben had seen out in the deeper water. Had they come in close, disoriented by the storm like she was? Or had she drifted so far out that she was now fair game for the big predators? Her breathing was coming in pants now. Whatever it was bumped her again, and this time she screamed.

Dashing the water from her eyes she realized it was a plastic seat cushion, torn and muddied, probably blown loose from a boat. She grabbed on to it, dismayed when her clumsy fingers could not grip and the cushion slipped from her grasp. With her last supply of strength she heaved herself at it. This time her fingers cooperated and she wrapped her arms around tight. The cushion held, keeping her torso mostly above the water. Panting hard, she clung to the foam, grateful that one small thing had gone right, feeling the exquisite comfort of having something support her in the endless expanse of ocean. Cheek pressed to the sodden fabric, she rested until she felt the strength to raise her head again.

She saw no sign of Leland. The conditions would prohibit her from making them out anyway. Perhaps he and Martin had decided to make a last-ditch effort to reach the mainland, though with the storm raging she did not see how they could have completed the trip.

Ahead loomed the spit of land, crowded with scraggly mangroves. She pushed hard in that direction but found she did not make any progress. The cushion was both a help and a hindrance, keeping her from pulling her way through the water. She did not dare let go as she knew she did not have the strength to keep herself afloat without it.

In spite of her kicking and one-armed thrashing, she could not correct course. The spit of land loomed in front of her, but the waves were rushing past at such a furious pace she knew she would be swept by.

You will not give up, she repeated to herself one last time, the clashing water drowning out her thoughts.

SIXTEEN

Reuben fought to keep his footing as he neared the lagoon, straining to see through the deluge. There was no sign of Antonia. The skimmer was caught on its side among the trees, also empty. He splashed out into the water, listening to the waves increasing in violence as they pounded the outer edge of the trees, trying to piece together what had happened.

"Antonia!" he shouted, but the wind snatched the words away. They'd tried for the mainland? But the skimmer would not be wedged in the lagoon. They'd sought shelter? Where? Only two choices—the boathouse where they might have stored some gear…or the lighthouse.

He didn't know how long it might take Silvio, Gavin and Paula to make it to the Anchor, but they'd be slow since Gavin was wounded. Would they arrive to find Leland and his buddy waiting? Reuben's gut throbbed with indecision. Some instinct deep down told him Antonia was nearby, but how could he find her with Tony slamming into the island?

He took the slope to the Anchor at a run, but his efforts left him struggling against the raging tumult that shrieked around him and shoved him back. Bent almost double, he plowed ahead, inching his way up the path one agonizing step at a time until he crested the slope. A tree hurtled by and he ducked aside, the branches thwacking into his burned shoulder. Above his position another half mile was the lighthouse and below, the panorama of the enraged ocean, slamming against the spit of land as if it meant to detach Isla from its moorings and pitch it loose.

Then he saw it.

The sizzle of lightning caught something in the water.

His eyes could not make out the details, but his heart knew. Panic filling every space inside him, he plunged off the path, through the grass and branches that clawed at his clothing until he burst through to the rock-strewn sand. Much of the spit was now underwater except for the highest spine of rock just visible still above the cresting sea. And that's where he saw her again, head bobbing, arms wrapped around something as she was being swept past the outcropping.

He ran until his feet found no more surface to support them. Then he swam, body thrashing against the power of the hurricane as he struck out toward her, trying to call her name, deluged every time he opened his mouth. The wave walls obscured his vision and he lost her.

Nee, his mind screamed. *Show me where you are.*

Another crest picked him up, raising him to impossible heights before hurling him down. It was enough. He got the tiniest glimpse of her and struck out again, body fueled by a strength he hadn't known he possessed.

A new series of waves worked to pull him apart from her, but he fought his way back. Every sinew in his arms and back protested as he battled his way forward until finally he grabbed the pink collar of her shirt.

Her arms were clutched tightly around whatever she was holding.

"Nee!" he shouted.

She did not answer. Her face was dead white and rigid with fear or cold or both. He didn't waste any more time orienting himself between the crest of one wave and the trough of another. They were not that far from the shore, but the spit was now almost entirely underwater due to the storm surge. The flood was carrying them too fast, near enough to the shore that he could swim, but not while he was clinging tight to Antonia. If he didn't make it to land soon they would be swept past and drowned in open water.

The rocks were both tantalizing and terrifying, promising rescue from drowning, or death from being crushed against them as the waves had their way. He kicked as hard as he could toward the only small area he could see that was still above the waterline.

It did no good. The waves were strong. Too strong. Every ounce of energy he had left was going into holding on and trying to keep them afloat. His arms burned with the effort, and he found it increasingly difficult to continue treading water.

Despair began to crowd his mind. Still he kept kicking, trying to cut through the inexorable power of the surf. Through eyes blurred by salt water, he made out the figure of a man who appeared suddenly on the spit as if he'd risen up from the island itself.

He shouted, then stopped. Leland? He could not tell. Something splashed into the water, a blackened gas can with a rope tied around the handle. He lurched for it, but the can was sucked out of view. Treading water in agonizing circles, he looked again. No can, no rope. It must have been reeled in by the man on the spit.

Another splash and this time he grabbed the can, losing his grip on Antonia. She cried out and he let go of the can and went after her until he got hold of her wrist. The cushion pulled away and went careening past the rocks. She fought against the water, trying to move toward him, unable to beat back the surge. He clamped his other hand around her wrist, and she clung to him now, fingers digging into his flesh.

"Move with me," he shouted.

She thrust her legs and he did the same, and they inched up the spit until the gas can landed again. This time Antonia managed to snag her leg around the rope. He felt like shouting with elation, but he hadn't the breath.

He waited until she had grabbed the rope with both hands. Kicking to assist the man on the beach, they were pulled foot by agonizing foot onto the rocky point, where he found himself gazing up at the grimacing face of Gavin Campbell and his brother, Hector.

Antonia was hauled from the water by unseen hands until she collapsed on the slick black rock. As much as she longed to stay prone on that hard surface, part of her brain knew the entire spit would be submerged in a matter of moments. She felt a hand on her arm, pulling her up, but her knees would not hold. Somehow Gavin was there, shoving his shoulder under Reuben's, and then someone lifted her and she was being held by a set of strong arms and being carried away from the water.

She looked up into the face of Hector Sandoval. She must be dreaming. She'd survived the ocean to be delivered into the hands of the man who had arranged the whole nightmare. *Get away. Fight for your life.* Though her brain knew what to do, her body would not cooperate. Escaping from his hold was not possible, as she had not one tiny iota of strength left. Helpless as a rag doll, she let herself be carried away from the spit, toward the sheltering arms of the nearest tiny pocket of lagoon.

There Hector put her down and Reuben collapsed to the ground beside her, panting, on the wet fringe of mud that wasn't taken up by the stiltlike roots of the mangroves.

Gavin and Hector crouched low to avoid the screaming wind that howled over the tops of the trees. Gavin's face was drawn with pain, eyes smudged underneath with shadow.

"That impromptu rescue doesn't change anything!" Gavin hollered at Hector.

Hector shot him a bitter smile. "You will have your pound of flesh, Agent Campbell, after I get mine. Leland is still here. I saw him go to the boathouse just before the eye passed."

"That w-w-was right after he tried to drown me," she chattered.

Hector might have replied though she could not be sure over the roar.

Reuben took Antonia's hand. She felt the pressure of his fingers, but the cold was so deep she could not feel his skin on hers.

Gavin's eyes narrowed at Hector. "Is that why you took off from the lighthouse after we arrived?"

"Did you think I was running from you?" Hector shouted. "Don't flatter yourself. I was going to find Leland, and on my way I saw these two." He turned his gaze back on Reuben. "Whatever you think of me, I never set out to hurt anyone. I really did change my life, brother, but the past came back stronger than ever." He threw a hand toward the sky. "Just like this storm."

"Don't make it worse," Reuben gasped, sides heaving.

Hector smiled and touched his brother on the shoulder. "Worse? How could any of this possibly get worse?" Then he sprinted out of the mangroves and disappeared.

Gavin moved to follow.

"You can't catch him," Reuben said.

Gavin gave him a cocky grin. "You grow oranges. I stop bad guys. Let's stick to our own jobs, shall we?" he said, getting painfully to his feet, doubled over under the onslaught. "Can you get back to the lighthouse by yourselves? Silvio and Paula are there already."

Silvio and Paula? Relief billowed inside, warming her a fraction. They'd survived Leland's assault and escaped the fire.

Antonia didn't have the energy to nod to Gavin, but Reuben must have because Gavin headed in the direction Hector had taken a moment before. She could not process what had happened; her brain was reeling, battered like her body. She tried to get up, but her knees would not allow it.

"We'll rest here, just for a little while," he said in her ear, and she thought she'd never heard such sweet words in all her life. Thoughts and emotions roiled through her body in such a crazy kaleidoscope that she could not arrange a coherent thought.

Reuben moved next to her and they eased down, backs propped against the welcoming arms of the mangroves, his body curled around hers, his arms chafing some small warmth back into her deadened limbs.

"I love you, Antonia," she heard him say. Or was it the strange echo of a long-ago memory, dredged up by the hurricane? Imagination? Or her heart's desire?

The wind, the storm, Hector, Leland, the fire. It all faded away in the wake of that touch. "Reuben, I want…I want…" But the rest would not come, not even to her own mind. Tears began to pour from her eyes. He gathered her closer, and she felt the change in him. Where his body had been so cold a moment before, it now began to warm as he pressed her to his chest.

"Just rest, Nee," he spoke into her ear. "Just rest." Then somehow she'd turned and his lips were pressed against hers, teasing the life back into her.

She could not see the lagoon for the tears; she could not hear the hurricane over the tumult of her own heartbeat. There was only the feel of Reuben's kiss, his strong embrace and the profound sense of gratitude that she was alive to experience it once more.

Reuben's eyes blinked open. He'd been dreaming about a perfect kiss, and sparks still danced through his limbs. Disorientation buzzed his brain until a myriad of strange sensations brought him up to speed; the press of the hard mangrove roots in his back, the discomfort of waterlogged clothes and the supreme thrill of Antonia's head lying against his chest, which drove all the other details away except for one. Water lapped at his legs.

He sat up too quickly and she woke, face blurred with confusion.

"Water's rising. We've got to move," he urged. The rain was still falling, though perhaps not as violently, he thought, winds still howling and the lagoon was indeed flooding. He took her hand and they struggled free from the mangrove roots and back toward the trail that led to the lighthouse. On the way he berated himself for allowing them to linger so long. The lower part of the trail was under two feet of water, which they splashed through. Antonia kept up as well as she could, but he knew she was exhausted both mentally and physically. Her motions were stumbling and awkward.

He wanted to carry her, to ease something of the

burden he'd created, but she would never allow it. He had to get her to shelter, to rest and to some water and food. The storm was weakening, or perhaps that was wishful thinking, and now it was a waiting game. Could they last until help finally arrived?

As he took her hand to help her over another fallen log, he heard her suck in a breath. They both froze as the glossy armored body of an alligator slithered by, half swimming and half waddling where there was debris to support his massive ten-foot body. The animal cast them a glance with its small protruding eyes as if weighing the effort it would require to go after one of them. Reuben knew this guy, had seen him many times while prowling the lagoons with Hector. With a fifty-year life span, it might be the same critter his mother had written about in her journals, naming him Cazador, hunter.

He was not hunting now, Reuben knew. Alligators didn't run prey down on land; they hunkered quietly in the water, waiting for that easy meal. One giant snap, one or two massive swallows, that was the alligator's way. Humans would be far too much work. Still a threatened alligator was a ferocious beast with eighty-odd teeth and a bite force of two thousand pounds.

Antonia shivered next to him. Animal lover that she was, alligators scared her, always had.

"He's not hunting," Reuben said, "just trying to get back to the lagoon. He's after shelter, like we are."

She nodded and gave him a wobbly smile. "Wish I had his waterproof skin."

That tenuous smile seemed more precious at that moment than anything he'd ever possessed in his whole life. He held it in his mind as the alligator cleared the way and slithered into the deeper water at the bottom of the trail. Suddenly, Reuben's body moved of its own accord, pulling her close, pressing kisses along her temple and down her neck. He heard her gasp, and he could not bottle up the words as he let the memories of their fight against the surf thunder through him.

"Nee, if anything happened to you, if you were lost…" he mumbled into the sweet place where the pulse throbbed in her throat. Emotions long suppressed exploded through him, sparking trails of longing that started in his stomach and spread through his soul as he savored the feel of her.

She pulled away from him, her eyes enormous in her pale face.

He sucked in a breath, trying to read her expression.

She took his hands between her own and squeezed tightly. "Thank you for swimming out there to get me. You could have died, too."

And with that string of words, she put their relationship back into clear focus again. *Reuben, she doesn't love you anymore and she can't get over the past.* Pain cut deep and he took a step back, trying to control his breathing, to put the storm of feeling back into the bottle where it would stay except on quiet sun-drenched mornings when he would stand on the beach and watch the morning paint the sky without her.

He cleared his throat and pretended to examine the horizon. "I think the worst is nearly over," he said as the cold rain slapped him in the face.

She didn't reply as they climbed over the log. The next few feet of trail was pinched in on either side by thick screens of shrubbery and mounded debris. Reuben struck out in front, forging through water that was up to his knees. Cold seeped deep inside, cooling his bones and chilling his blood.

What had he expected? That she would decide to forget the past when his brother had nearly gotten them all killed? Stupid, but he'd never been smart where she was concerned. He'd just let his heart lead him.

Try using your head for a change, Reuben. Survive this storm, why don't you? Debris swirled through the water ahead of him. He bent to push a piece of jagged plaster aside when a gunshot whistled over his shoulder.

SEVENTEEN

Antonia did not register the noise as quickly as Reuben did. He carried her down into the water as another shot cut through the rain. Scrabbling to the edge of the path, they ran into the shrubbery, plunging down a slope that led back to the lagoon.

She caught the sound of branches breaking behind her. A shot whacked off the top of a water-soaked branch next to her ear as she slipped and slid until they were deep in the mangroves again, water up to their armpits, the canopy closing over their heads. She had no idea where they were headed. So intent was she on where the next shot would come from that the water took her by surprise, deepening into a dark, cold pocket that forced her to tread water to keep her chin above it.

The thought of being stuck in deep water again awakened a trail of terror inside her. She wanted to call out to stop him, but Reuben kept on slowly inching deeper into the mangroves until even the sound of the ocean was muffled by the eerie growth.

"Where are we going?" she whispered as he finally pulled himself up on a curved root and helped her scramble next to him, her feet still resting in the water.

"He can't shoot us if he's swimming," Reuben murmured back. "Who is it?"

Antonia slung the wet hair out of her face. "Leland's little helper, Martin. I think they've decided we need to die since we're all witnesses now and we didn't cooperate with the drowning plan."

Water sparkled on Reuben's stubbled chin. "Must have split up when they figured out we'd survived."

Antonia watched the leaves shivering around her, each set dancing by the rain. The smell of vegetation tickled her nose. "If the storm's slowing, then the coast guard will come back, so they'll need to finish before that happens." She swallowed. "What do we do now?"

Reuben wiped at his face. "These mangroves are all connected, more or less. If we keep covered, we can circle back and set a signal fire maybe, get the coast guard's attention sooner rather than later." He offered her a wan smile. "You know, like they did in the days before cell phones."

Antonia found herself smiling back. Something still fluttered inside her from Reuben's kisses, as if the warmth of them lingered on her skin, though her teeth were chattering madly. She'd wanted to give in to the emotion that poured from him then, to forget everything but the sweetness that he offered up at that moment, but something stopped her.

The litany of hurts poured through her in a river of bitter memory.

Anger at Reuben and his brother for turning her life upside down.

Confusion that she could still feel the strong current of tenderness while the painful past replayed over and over in her mind.

Fear still fresh and ferocious at her near drowning only hours before, and now the added terror of Martin's relentless efforts. Reuben interrupted her thoughts. He climbed up farther into the mangrove canopy and scouted for their pursuer. "I don't see him."

Tiny fish bumped against Antonia's ankles below the murky water. At least, she wanted to believe the motion was caused by the tiny fish that used the sheltering mangrove roots as a nursery of sorts, protection from the larger predators until they were big enough to venture into open waters. Surely it would not be the alligator, hunkered down in a mud pocket, waiting for the storm to subside.

She climbed farther up the arms of the mangrove tree next to Reuben. "Where do you think Martin is?" she whispered.

He didn't answer. A flock of birds suddenly erupted from the branches to their left, long necks stretched dark against the sky, wide wings fanning the storm-tossed air. Reuben leaped from the tree and she followed, plunging once again into the lagoon. The sound must have alerted Martin because the bushes thrashed as he pursued them.

"Tired of this," Martin bellowed. "Sick of this storm and this island."

Reuben forced his way through the mangroves, making sure she was right behind him. Leaves slapped at her face, spangling water down her neck. There was no land underneath their feet, only the clawed roots that enabled the mangroves to thrive in the constant ebb and flow of the tide. They climbed over roots and squeezed under the ones that left enough clearance. Finding a foothold underneath the surface of the green water was impossible.

She stumbled, and he held her up by her hand. They made their clumsy way along, feet slipping in their haste.

Suddenly they found themselves stopped by an impenetrable wall of mangrove roots woven in a tight latticework, hemming them in the tiny circle of water like two caught fish. Martin could be no more than a couple of yards behind them.

Breath tight with terror, she realized they could not make it through those interwoven roots before he caught them.

Reuben went down in the water so abruptly she thought he must have fallen. She thrashed around for him, not daring to call out his name.

Her fingertips found his shoulder just as he erupted from the water, brown eyes wide.

"We can get through. There's a channel."

Through the cloudy water she could make out the dark shadow, a gap in the roots no bigger than a manhole cover. Desperately she looked around for some way, any way, to avoid submerging herself again, but there was only the wall of mangrove and the sound of Martin crashing toward them.

Reuben held out his hand.

She locked eyes on his.

I'm afraid to trust you, her mind whispered.

There was a sheen of yearning in his eyes, the naked emotion that told her he wanted nothing more than her well-being, yet her heart had been torn apart already when she'd given it to him. He wanted forgiveness, and though she knew it was required, extended to her in endless heavenly grace, she hesitated.

"I'm going to kill you both," Martin hollered again, and the leaves shook around them from his wild thrashing.

She looked once more into Reuben's face, his offered hand, the plea for her trust just one more time.

In spite of the warnings rattling through her, she knelt next to him and watched as he vanished into the dank hole. Heaving in one more very deep breath, Antonia sank to her knees and squeezed in after him, the enveloping water muffling the sound of the shots fired just behind her.

Reuben's lungs burned as he peered through the tea-colored water to find a gap big enough for them to emerge. Perhaps he had miscalculated and they would have to return and face Martin. Thirty seconds, forty-five, and the network of roots seemed even more impenetrable, caging them under the surface. Behind him he felt Antonia's movements grow more frantic. Where had he seen the patch of sunlight that pointed the way to escape? He could not—would not—fail Antonia again. Finally he spotted the clearing through which the sunlight shone a pale yellow.

He exploded upward, sucking in a lungful of air and turning to be sure Antonia had surfaced behind him. She did, coughing and spluttering. "He's still shooting," she gasped.

He pulled himself out of the water and balanced on the stiltlike roots, helping her up next to him. They'd emerged in a long ribbon of lagoon not more than two feet across, hedged in by the walls of mangrove.

"We can make our way along this channel," he whispered.

"He'll follow."

"We're quicker."

"You think so?"

He flashed a smile. "Remember the races on the beach?" She did; he could tell by the softening in her face. Endless sprints down Isla's glorious pristine beaches. The reward for his win? A kiss. The reward for hers? The same. He had not realized then exactly how precious those kisses were. He knew now how rare and fragile love could be, and he meant to sacrifice everything to the last breath if it would keep Antonia alive.

Agile as they both were, exhaustion, dehydration and hunger would work against them. Martin was likely suffering from none of those conditions, and he still had the upper hand while he still had bullets or Leland came to join him. The branches were slick as they made their awkward way along, like two people walking a tightrope of roots. The wind was definitely weaker now and the rain reduced to a constant drizzle. They'd survived Tony.

Would they survive Martin and Leland?

Picking their way to the water's edge, they slipped in. The depth was some ten feet, he estimated, swollen from the storm surge and the torrential rain. Proper swimming was not an option as the surface was cluttered with broken tree limbs and heaps of leaves that swirled in massive clumps. They settled for a sort of modified crawl, kicking along and pushing the detritus out of their way as they went.

His stomach growled, and he tried to remember how long it was since he'd eaten, but he was not entirely sure even what day it was. They stopped to listen for Martin but heard nothing other than the rustling leaves. His arms ached from the constant battle against obstacles, but he didn't complain and neither did Antonia.

Fish swirled in the water underneath them, bumping into his legs occasionally, and a turtle poked his head out of the water before disappearing again. On the positive side, the might of the hurricane had passed. Now the lagoon dwellers were emerging from their hiding places. He hoped Leland would not do the same, at least until they escaped the present danger.

The channel twisted and looped around, crisscrossed by large channels, which they avoided, and smaller ones. It was like navigating a giant living labyrinth, but now the sun was visible and he was able to get a sense of their direction.

"Where are we going?" Antonia said, rousing him from his thoughts.

He turned to reply and her face took the words straight from his mind. Daylight showed how badly the previous hours had treated her. Her chin was barely above the water, her face pale and scratched. Dark smudges under her eyes revealed the extent of her exhaustion, and she was shivering, though the day was warming rapidly. It had to have been hours since she'd had any water, longer still since she'd eaten, and bruises on her arms and cheeks showed how cruelly she'd been battered by the ocean.

He floated over to her. "This channel joins the creek about a half mile from here."

"We can get to land?" she asked weakly.

"Yes, real soon. Tired?"

She nodded.

"Piggyback ride?" He didn't exactly wait for a response, just offered his back, grateful when she wrapped her arms around his shoulders and her knees around his waist and he began to tow her along. She did not resist, allowing herself to be moved gently against the water, her head mostly leaning against his back, sometimes turning to scan for any sign of Martin.

They moved slower now, her added weight making it harder for him to navigate the debris, but he knew she could not struggle along on her own much longer. Another turn in the channel and he felt the water change, growing colder, the current moving more rapidly. The river. He'd been right in his calculations.

The mangroves thinned out and spindly shrubs poked here and there through the roots, some nearly denuded of their leaves. He felt the bottom under his feet as they made the final turn.

The creek and lagoon water were now a swirling cauldron that lapped all the way up to the cabbage palms, and it was several yards farther before they finally made it clear of the water altogether. Antonia slipped off his back and they slogged up the submerged bank, sinking into the mud. Each step was an effort as they pulled free from the sucking ooze.

He gathered her close behind the cabbage palms and allowed them both a moment to catch their breath. Antonia's whole body was shaking now, and she clung to him.

"My legs aren't working," she whispered.

"We'll use mine then," he murmured back, hoisting her in his arms, noting she had lost her shoes somewhere in the cloying mud. His mind whirled as he considered their next move. There was no way to know if Martin had given up the pursuit somewhere. Martin or no Martin, he had to get Antonia into some sort of shelter, but what was left intact? The lighthouse was probably the best bet, but he could not ask her to walk there until she'd rested and he would not be able to carry her all the way since half the island was now underwater.

The bungalow.

It was time to find out if the expensive storm retrofits had done their job. He began the slow ascent to the hill where the bungalow sat, praying all the while it was not under several feet of ocean. Antonia didn't say a word as they traveled, nestled limply in his arms, which made him worry all the more.

Skirting a pile of windblown wood he recognized as part of the Isla Hotel's upper balcony, he made his way up the sodden slope until the roof of the bungalow came into view.

The relief he felt at finding the structure intact and not submerged made him want to shout. Instead he pressed forward until they reached the front walk and Antonia wriggled out of his grasp.

He found the floor covered by a good four inches of water. It hardly mattered. The tiny cottage had a roof and four walls and right now that was better than a fine palace.

Inside, the bed frame was lapped by water, the bedding soaked. Sloshing in, he stripped off the wet blankets until the mattress was covered only by the plastic protector, which he silently thanked Paula for insisting on. "Climb aboard," he said. He expected a funny remark or a hesitation, but he got none of those. She meekly climbed up on the mattress. There was no dry pillow to be found, but Antonia curled up on her side and closed her eyes.

He went outside and shimmied open one set of storm shutters, allowing some sunlight to enter. They could now see out, which made him feel marginally better. Back inside he shoved the door closed but found the wood so swollen with water that it would not lock. After a full five minutes of scanning for any possible sign of Martin, he turned away from the window. Splashing quietly so as not to wake Antonia, he floundered into the kitchen. Everything in the lower cupboards was floating around the water-covered tile floor. There was nothing much to be salvaged. Some of the upper cupboards had been snatched open by the wind that had plowed in, but somehow one was left closed.

He squeaked it open. Inside was a six-pack of pineapple juice. He resisted the urge to whoop for joy. Continued prowling produced a plastic jar of peanuts, which plunked against his shins as he waded around. With the seal still intact, the contents were neatly preserved. Though his mouth watered at the thought of food, he stacked the treasure on the kitchen counter and stripped the saturated cushions off of a wooden chair, setting it into position by the front window and climbing up, seating himself cross-legged to keep his feet out of the water. The only thing he could find to offer for protection besides the knife in its sheath on his belt was a broken chair rail, and he laid this across his lap. Though he meant to keep watch for the slightest sign of Martin's approach, his gaze kept wandering to Antonia.

Her dark lashes fluttered against her cheeks, and he hoped she was not dreaming about what had happened in the past few days. His thoughts drifted back to his brother for the first time since he'd left the lighthouse. His stomach clenched in anger. Though Reuben had tried to ignore the truth, Hector saw it clear as sunrise—Reuben had never stopped loving Antonia.

Hector exploited that vulnerability in his brother

to save his own skin. And what was the cost of his decision? Gavin was shot. Reuben's boats ruined. A sadistic gangster roved the ruins, determined to pursue them at any cost.

In the distance he could just make out the broken outline of the Isla Marsopa Hotel, his mother's dream, reduced to rubble. Suddenly none of it mattered, and he could not remember why he had fought so hard to keep things intact. Maybe it was the pride he felt, the aura of righteousness at holding together something of their mother's. He'd gone through the motions, the money, the toil to try to save a building—a collection of wooden beams and nails, nothing more—when the one thing he'd wanted, craved, in fact, was to save his brother. How he'd prayed, how he'd scolded, reprimanded, pleaded and berated. For nothing.

People don't save people, do they, Lord? Salvation is Yours to give and Yours alone. Something like peace settled into his soul at that moment. He would love his brother until his dying breath, and he would pray that Hector would earnestly repent, but it was Hector's choice to make and he would have to decide what kind of man he was going to be if they survived.

Reuben's choice, his only choice, was to ask God to intercede and keep Antonia alive.

With one last look at her face, relaxed and peaceful in sleep, he clenched his hands in prayer.

EIGHTEEN

Antonia didn't remember climbing up onto that mattress or falling asleep, but sunlight on her face awakened her what must have been several hours later. Her lashes felt gummy, her mouth dry, and for a moment she did not recall how she'd gotten to be napping on a stripped mattress with water sloshing gently around her. Rays of golden light peeked through the window where the storm shutter had been partially opened, dispelling some of the gloom in the bungalow.

Reuben sat on a wooden chair, a piece of rail across his lap, staring out the window. Seeing him there brought a crush of emotions all at once. What did he see as he gazed out at what was left of Isla? Ruined dreams? The betrayal of a brother he'd trusted steadfastly? She could not read the expression on his face, but she thought it might have been sorrow, and the need to comfort blossomed in her heart, strong and solid. Before the hurricane she would have ignored the feeling. Now, it seemed, the hurricane had stripped away some of the hardness that calloused her, but she did not know quite how to act on the strange feelings. "Still raining?"

He jerked toward her, a smile now transforming his face. "Hey, there. I'm glad you're awake. The rain has stopped finally, winds are dying down and somehow the island isn't totally underwater. We made it through Tony."

"I wonder if we'll make it through Leland," she couldn't help but add.

"We'll make it, but one thing at a time." He wedged the chair against the door and waded to the kitchen, returning and presenting her with a can of pineapple juice and a jar of peanuts. "Ta-da!" he trumpeted.

She goggled. "You found food!" It came out in a high-pitched squeal.

"Didn't you order room service, madam?" He feigned confusion. "I'm sorry. I'll just take this back to the kitchen."

"No way," she giggled, snatching the peanuts from his hands.

They popped the tops off the pineapple juice and drained two cans each. He peeled off the foil seal of the peanut jar and poured her a massive handful before filling his own palm. They gobbled the salty nuts, eating until they had emptied the container.

Antonia's eyes closed in pleasure. "Of all the meals I've eaten in my life, I think that was the best."

"Certainly the finest company," he added.

She blushed. "Considering we're stranded on an island with only a few other people, several of whom are killers, that's not saying much."

He laughed and held a pineapple can out in a toast. "To the finest meal the Isla Hotel has ever produced. And the last," he added, more quietly.

Her smile dimmed as she clinked his can with hers. "Can it be restored, do you think? Isla, I mean?"

His lips pressed together and something went dull in his eyes. "You know the answer to that."

She did and it pained her deep down so she sought another subject. "Is there any more food?"

"What, still hungry?" he said, hopping off the mattress and splashing into the kitchen.

"Not now, but I will be soon," she said.

He dumped the contents of a small grocery bag onto the counter. "I found a couple of useful things. Two granola bars," he said, wiggling them for her to see. "A box of matches, which looks to be relatively dry. Three bandages and a flashlight that doesn't work right now but might once it dries out." He regarded her triumphantly. "What do you think?"

"Not as magnificent as the peanuts, but those granola bars will come in handy later." She shivered. "I'd give a pretty penny to have some dry clothes right about now."

"Sorry, can't help you with that one. The washer and dryer have done their last loads." He stopped, then shook his head. "Thought I heard a helicopter. Wishful thinking."

"When do you think the coast guard will come back?"

He drifted to the window and peered out. "Not anytime soon unless we can convince them there's an emergency situation here. They've got plenty bigger priorities right now."

Dread kindled inside her. "How will we do that? Are the phones working?"

"No, but I've been thinking if I could get to the skimmer, providing it's still afloat, there's a radio in it. If it's intact, I could call for help."

The thought of going back to that spot in the lagoon where she'd been marched out to drown made her feel sick. She swallowed hard. "Okay. I'm in."

"No. I'll go myself, but first we need to regroup for a while and maybe get Silvio and Paula back here if we can. They'll need to rest, and Silvio can help secure the doors. Either that or we get you to the lighthouse and wait for help there. Neither place is great, but it's all that's still standing except for the boathouse."

"What about Hector and Gavin?" she asked softly. "They were headed to the boathouse."

"I don't know what to do about that." He looked at her. "I don't know how to help my brother. I never did."

"You loved him the best way you could."

He didn't answer, turning instead to gaze out the window again.

The light picked up the deep shadows on his face, lines of fatigue engraving his forehead. "Reuben, why don't you lie down now? I'll take a turn watching."

"I'm okay."

"No, you're not. You're exhausted and you need to rest. I had my turn, it's yours now." She hopped off the bed and sloshed over to him. "Rest, just for a few minutes. Please."

He shook his head. "I want to be ready if he comes."

She touched a finger to a long scratch on his temple, tracing the line down the side of his face. His eyes closed and he caught her hand in his, pressing it to his face, lips seeking the place at her wrist where her pulse hammered at his touch. Then she was in his arms, holding him close, stroking his back as if she could smooth away the past and restore what had been taken from him, from them both.

"I'm sorry," she whispered, "that everything is ruined here on Isla."

He sighed, warm breath ruffling her hair. "I wasn't meant to be here, running this hotel, Nee. My pride told me I was the one, the only one who could save it, and that gave me some kind of self-importance, I guess. God wants me in an orange field, tending those trees. He's been telling me that all along. I should have listened." He pressed his face into the crook of her neck. "I should have listened to a lot of things."

They clung to each other. "I've made mistakes, too, Reuben."

He raised his head then, and she saw moisture glimmering in his eyes. "But your mistakes didn't wreck things."

Didn't they? Hadn't her relentless need to expose Hector's failings driven further the wedge between them? Her decision to support her sister's flight, helping her keep Gracie away from Hector, had also removed the little girl from Reuben, from this uncle who loved her desperately. Had running been the only answer? But at the very core of her being she knew her greatest sin—that she had not wanted Hector proved innocent, but condemned.

"If it means anything at all," Reuben said, "my brother said he has been clean for the past five years. He was blackmailed back in by the Garzas. They threatened him with prison and never seeing Gracie again if he didn't deliver Isla."

And you believe that? The thought sprang to her mind, but she swallowed it. "I'm sorry. I know you love your brother."

He gave her a startled look, followed by the sweetest smile she had ever seen, one that went right past her defenses, the regret and condemnation straight into her soul. She stroked his cheek, and he pressed close to her, his mouth inches from her own.

A snap sounded from outside.

Reuben raced to the front window and she crowded next to him.

"I don't see anything," she whispered.

"I don't, either, but that noise was close. We'd better move."

Stuffing the last two cans of juice into his pockets along with the granola bars, he pushed her toward the back door, which hung crookedly on its hinges, wedged in place against the concrete porch step. The gap was only a scant twelve inches across, and though Antonia slipped easily through, Reuben's broad shoulders wedged.

"Go," he hissed. "Run to the woods along the creek. Head for the lighthouse."

"No way. You're coming, or I'm not going," she whispered back.

"Nee, move it," he commanded.

She did not budge except to take his hand and yank as hard as she could until he finally stumbled clear of the door. Then they were running, heads down, as quietly as they could manage into the cover of the mangled palms and trees.

Pushing through the wet branches brought them close to the swollen banks of the creek, which lapped the very top and spilled over. The ground was treacherous with debris and slippery rocks, but they kept up a quick pace until they were a good fifty yards from the bungalow. Ahead on the ridge sat the wreck of the hotel, some patches of white paint shining oddly in the sunlight. Panting and scratched they slowed to a halt.

Antonia pressed a hand to her cramping side. If she hadn't had a small rest and something to eat and drink, she never would have completed the run. As it was she was still fighting fatigue, her muscles rubbery and weak and her bare feet painfully battered. She wondered how Reuben was holding up.

He pulled her to the dripping canopy of an oak tree and climbed on a rock to peer back at the bungalow.

It was hard to know if they had made a reasonable choice fleeing from their only shelter. Were they both suffering from paranoia? Or had Martin found his way out of the mangroves and tracked them to the bungalow?

"I don't see any sign of him," Reuben said. "Maybe I was wrong."

"No you weren't," Martin said, stepping from the shrubbery and firing his gun at Reuben.

The sound of the gunshot nearly deafened Reuben, and he felt the hot metal skimming by his shirtsleeve. Antonia screamed. Grabbing a stout, fallen branch, he swung it at Martin. "Run, Antonia," he hollered. "Get away from here."

Instead of running, she picked up a rock and heaved it, missing Martin by several feet. She picked up another and another, hurling them at him with rapid-fire motion, eyes wild and hair flying. Martin batted most of them away with his free hand, but one or two struck his shoulder and he swung the gun at her.

It was as if Reuben were in the grip of a living nightmare. There was a gun pointed at Antonia. It was the most vicious, ugly scenario he could imagine, and it filled him with pure fury that scorched a white-hot path from his gut throughout every muscle in his body. Swinging the makeshift club with strength born of rage, he advanced on Martin, hitting him so hard the gun spiraled loose and skittered away into the mud.

Antonia scrambled after it, searching desperately through the grass with outstretched hands.

Martin howled, his face going red as Reuben readied for another strike with the branch. "What do you think you're doing, boy?" Martin rasped. "Think you're going to take me down with that stick?"

"That's exactly what I think," Reuben snarled.

"All right then. Let's see what you've got."

Reuben swung again, and Martin danced to the side before launching himself stomach down at Reuben's ankles. Sidestepping, Reuben meant to leap over Martin, but he skidded on the mucky ground and went down on one knee. Martin rolled over and grabbed Reuben's waist, bringing them both to the mud.

They grappled and rolled. Reuben tried to reach for the knife sheathed at his waist, but Martin's hands went around his throat and he had to apply all his strength to keep from being choked.

Antonia looked frantically from Reuben to the grass where she was still pawing for Martin's gun.

Finally able to pry Martin's fingers loose, Reuben shoved his foot into Martin's chest and sent him backward. Martin landed on his back, panting, sweat beading on his forehead. Slowly he rolled over and stood.

"Not bad for a farmer," Martin said. "But you're going to die anyway."

Reuben's heart pounded so hard the vibrations shuddered through his body. "Yep, but it's not going to be today," he breathed. "Not here and not now."

Martin smiled and hurled himself again at Reuben. This time, Reuben did avoid the collision, moving just enough that Martin stumbled to his knees. Reaching out, Reuben knew this time he could use his advantage to get around behind the guy and press him facedown to the ground.

His miscalculation became clear a moment later. Time seemed to slow as he realized that Martin had pulled a knife from his belt. There was no time to react as his arm arced and he plunged the knife forward. Reuben felt it grating against his ribs a second before the explosive pain. Through an excruciating haze he saw Antonia, who looked up just as the knife slid home, horror infusing her beautiful face, an odd contrast to the ugly triumph on display on Martin's.

Run, Nee, he wanted to shout, but he could not force his mouth to give voice to the words.

He staggered back and then he was falling, spiraling backward, hitting the swollen creek with a harsh smack. Water closed over his head, and through the silted depths he caught one more glimpse of Antonia before the creek whisked him away.

NINETEEN

"Reuben," she screamed, running to the edge of the creek. A flash of his arm, one tiny glimpse, and then he was gone, sucked under the roiling surface.

"Too bad," Martin said, brushing off the soiled knees of his pants. "He shoulda stayed in the fields. Farmers almost never get themselves drowned." He chuckled.

Antonia wanted to scream, to beat at his awful chest, but she was numb with horror as she stared at the spot where Reuben had been only a second before. *Reuben, Reuben,* her mind wailed. Martin grabbed her by the arm and pulled her roughly away from the creek. She tried to twist out of his grasp. Reuben could make it to shore, and she could help him climb out. Her feet turned back toward the rushing water, but Martin forced her away.

"He's gone. We'll go to Leland and see what he wants to do with you." She could not form a coherent thought marching across the soggy ground. Everything was a numbing void.

She tripped over a broken slab of plaster and he jerked her up by the back of her shirt. She had to get away from him, to get back to the creek. The water would have carried Reuben downstream toward the lagoon. It was quieter there, tranquil. He could get out; she would help him. Her mind spun frantically.

"We called for help," she lied to Martin. "The coast guard is on its way."

He didn't answer at first. "Save your breath. You don't have a working phone. Not after both of you took your dip in the ocean."

"We radioed."

"With what?" he snorted.

"The radio on the skimmer."

Martin grabbed her elbow and turned her around. He was breathing heavily, and she was happy to note one of her rock missiles had found its mark on his cheek. "Radio's busted. We disconnected it."

"Reuben fixed it." She held her gaze steady, willing him to believe her ruse.

His eyes narrowed. "I don't think so."

"Well you'll believe it when they show up here." She searched the sky. "Shouldn't be too much longer. You saw the helicopter they sent just before the storm surge."

Breath held, she waited.

Martin considered. "All right, I'm game. We'll check the skimmer. If you're telling the truth, we'll radio again, tell them everything's fine. And if you're lying..." He smiled. "Then we can take our time and tie things up here properly."

She tried to think of a secondary plan as they went along. Somewhere on the path to the lagoon, she'd get away from him and find Reuben. Hardly a plan, hardly a chance.

Her stomach squeezed again and something cold slithered through her. She prayed that Reuben was not gravely hurt. He could not be. There was so much left she had to say. Martin huffed along the path, never more than a few feet behind her.

"Why do you do this?" she asked.

"What?"

"Abduction, murder, whatever Leland wants."

"Not Leland. Mr. Garza. He's my boss, and I do what he tells me."

She noted the sullen note that crept into his voice and filed that away to use to her advantage. "Killing innocent people, though? And women?"

"Don't usually kill women. Don't usually kill at all anymore. Too messy and attracts too much attention. This whole thing got out of hand, but you gotta do what you gotta do."

"Mr. Garza doesn't want you to kill us, does he? This is Leland's idea."

Martin's pace slowed for a moment. "Got no choice now. Mr. Garza will want things cleaned up."

"Are you sure about that?"

"What choice is there?" Martin huffed. "We got

an island full of witnesses now. You're going to have to die and that's that. Just a matter of how's best to do it."

"And you don't even have a qualm?" She shook her head. "No conscience that tells you what you're doing is wrong?"

"I don't get paid to have a conscience. Listen, honey, if you're looking for me to come to my senses and realize the error of my ways, it ain't gonna happen. Life's too short to worry about morals."

Too short not to. She sighed. "What a waste of a life."

Martin gave her a shove, which nearly sent her sprawling. "Just get going. All this talk is making my head ache."

They came to the deep pond of water, splashing in up to their knees and then down the muddy slope that led to the lagoon. "All these lagoons look the same to me," she said. "Do you remember where you stowed the skimmer?"

"Sure I do," he said, catching hold of her wrist. "Right down there, tied up safe."

The water made her slow and clumsy. There was no way she would escape even if she did manage to break the tight grip he had on her wrist.

Wait, Antonia. The moment will come. Watch for it. She wondered if Reuben had lost much blood from the stab wound. Was he still struggling against the rushing creek? The muscles in her chest knotted into a tight ball.

Martin did remember the pocket of lagoon where they had secured the skimmer. They made their ungainly way to the edge of the inlet, which was now showing signs of life again. Pushing aside the trailing Spanish moss, Martin peered into the little sanctuary. A pelican ruffled its feathers as if to shake off the remnants of the killer storm. Flickers in the surface indicated the fish, or perhaps it was the manatees, had begun to stir in the swollen circle of water. Martin had eyes for none of it. He thrashed forward, dragging her along until their feet sank in the muddy shore.

The skimmer was gone.

Perhaps it had blown loose in the surge. Martin must have considered that option, too, because he began to shove his way through the trees, heedless of the branches that slapped at them both.

They found the remnants of the rope, still knotted tightly around a sturdy tree trunk. Martin fingered the edge, which had been severed not by the power of the storm, but cut neatly with the aid of a knife.

Antonia stared at the cut rope. "Leland took the boat."

"No, that ain't what happened."

"Yes, it is," she argued. "He sent you out to find Reuben and me, and he took the skimmer and left. Left you behind."

"No," Martin barked. "He wouldn't do that."

"Oh, yes, he would," she breathed. "He decided things were too out of control here and he took off."

"It wasn't Leland," he snapped.

"Who then?" she demanded. "Couldn't have been me and you." She choked on the words. "You stabbed Reuben."

"The old man, then, or the cop. Maybe Hector."

"Silvio wouldn't leave his wife, and the cop has a bullet in his shoulder. He could hardly manage a boat by himself. Hector wouldn't leave his brother here to die." She was not sure it was true, but Martin's agitation was growing.

"Shut up," he said, grabbing her with both arms and shaking her until her head whipped back and forth. "He wouldn't leave me here to take the fall."

"Oh, yes, he would and you know it." She felt reckless, filled with a power she had no right to. "He could leave the country or go back to Garza and convince him it was all your idea to change the plan."

"Leland ain't gonna go and do something like that."

"Oh?" She spoke the next words softly, drilling them into him. "Why not? Life's too short to worry about morals." She thought she'd gone too far as his hands went for her throat. Instead he seized her arm again in a crushing grip.

"We're going to the boathouse. He'll be there."

And if he was? She knew she was playing a

dangerous game, and if she lost, her life, and Reuben's, would be forfeit.

Reuben was thrashed by the water, bumped and banged along by the creek until he somehow got a grip on a gnarled tree that protruded from the bank. His ribs burned, but he could not devote any energy into inspecting the wound. It took all his strength to wrap his arms and one leg around the root.

The bark was slippery as he tried to tug himself onto the tree, the rumbling water threatening to detach him at any moment. Agony lanced through his side as he fought. Martin would kill Antonia, or Leland would. The thought drove him to clench his cold fingers into claws that gripped the rough wood. He managed to pull himself clear of the water and he hung there now, like a bear cub stranded in a tree, panting and dripping, breath heaving and muscles screaming their displeasure.

He wanted to shimmy along to the bank. His body demanded oxygen instead so he hung there, staring upside down into the water, which seemed to be waiting for him to drop. After a full minute devoted just to breathing, he continued his awkward shimmy along the root, feeling the wood give and bend under his weight.

Another couple of feet and he would be close enough to try to grapple his way to shore. He kept his mind on Antonia, picturing her face. Though he was neither a painter nor a poet, his memory could render every detail—the silky strands of hair that she was apt to twist between fingers most always stained with paint, the radiant smile, the eyes that saw so much more than he ever could. Quick wit, quick temper, fast to find joy and first to embrace it. He brought up a memory of her laughing, the big belly guffaw that seemed incongruent with her slender body.

As he moved hand over hand, he replayed the sweetest images he'd filed away in his memory. Antonia swimming through a crystal sea. Antonia laughing as she inhaled the heady scent of the orange blossoms in his orchard. And yes, the moment when she'd walked away from him for the last time. Then, she had held up her chin, strength shining in her face, her lips trembling slightly. She loved him, but she would not turn her back on her sister or her niece for anyone, not even him. Maybe it was that moment, he thought, as he watched the water spin crazily underneath him, that he learned what a truly fine woman she was.

He felt the ominous snap, but there was nowhere to grab as the tree gave way and he was plunged again into the water. Landing on his back drove the breath out of him, and he struggled to right himself, breaking the surface and sucking in a mouthful of water in the process. He was being spun in circles, thrown up and down as he whirled along, unable to manage even one handhold on anything solid.

As it raced to empty itself into the sea, the creek hurtled through the trees so fast his vision blurred. He was weakening, teeth chattering, chin barely above the waterline, legs struggling to kick, arms no longer able to seek rescue. Helplessly, he felt himself being swept toward the lagoon. Perhaps there, in the slower water, in the sheltering arms of the lagoon that was a cradle for myriad creatures, he would also find refuge and a place to regroup.

If he could make it that far.

Ahead a curve of debris had collected in the creek, broken beams from Isla, sodden heaps of plaster and even a plastic cooler that had blown in from somewhere. It had all congealed into an unsightly pile that jutted out into the water. His heart leaped as he tried to gut his way through the waves toward the mass. His side was on fire, and he raked the pounding water until he managed to crook an elbow around a protruding two-by-four.

Choking and sputtering, he eased over the shifting debris, praying it would not break apart and deliver him into the mercy of the creek once again. Pieces of plaster shook loose under his feet, but the lattice of junk held firm until he heaved himself halfway out of the water. Clutching at the mud and straining forward, he found himself lying face down on the bank.

Thank You. It was all he could muster. He laid there heaving and coughing until he found the strength to roll over, the canopy of trees swimming in front of his eyes. Had he made it to the lagoon? Judging from the foliage he had not. The question became would he be able to manage it?

He reached a sitting position, though it cost him severe pain, and then rolled over onto his knees to try and lever himself into a stand. His gasping breaths were so noisy that he didn't hear anyone approach until a weathered hand was thrust into his face.

"Help ya up?" Silvio said.

Reuben goggled incredulously up at the man. "Silvio?"

"Who else would it be tramping around this place lookin' for you?" Silvio knelt next to Reuben and peered into his face, pale eyes scanning Reuben's shirtfront. "Someone got ya?"

"Martin. Didn't see the knife coming."

Silvio grunted. "Too slow. That's why you were never a good boxer."

"As I keep telling anyone who will listen, I'm a farmer, not a fighter."

Silvio chuckled as he hooked an arm under Reuben's shoulder. "Maybe not. Pretty good fight to get yerself out of the water."

Reuben could not hold in a groan of pain as Silvio raised him up.

"Come on," Silvio said. "Over here."

"Where's Paula?" Reuben grunted.

"You'll see soon enough. Be quiet and keep walkin'. I'm not too keen on having to carry you."

Reuben focused on walking, step by painful step, along the riverbank. Several times he had to stop, leaning against Silvio and struggling to stem the dizziness in his head. It seemed like miles before they came to the place where the river dumped itself into one of the lagoon channels, but it was likely no more than fifteen minutes' distance.

They stopped there and Reuben bent over, gasping for breath. When his head cleared enough for him to straighten again, he blinked at the unbelievable vision before him. It was the skimmer, bobbing gently on the waves, Paula perched inside, Charley the cat on her lap.

She shot to her feet, nearly falling in her haste to get to him, and Silvio handed her out of the boat.

Paula stopped abruptly in her dash toward him when she saw the blood that stained his shirtfront. Putting the cat down, she approached more slowly. "Come sit in the skimmer. There's a first-aid kit there."

With Silvio on one side and Paula on the other, Reuben was shuttled into the boat.

"How…?" he started.

Silvio shrugged. "Storm passed. We got tired of waiting for you or the bad guys to arrive. Went looking and found the skimmer. Decided we had better use for it than Leland."

Reuben grunted in pain when Paula peeled away the shirt from his side. "You should have gone for the mainland," he rasped.

"Not leaving you here. Or Antonia," he said. "Been trying to call the police, but my phone's out of juice."

Through gritted teeth Reuben fought the waves of burning pain as Paula swabbed the wound with an antiseptic wipe. "So we're still on our own."

"Looks that way." Silvio's gaze traveled over the storm-swollen lagoon. "What's the plan?"

"Find Antonia," he said.

Silvio raised an eyebrow. "Not much of a plan."

It's all that matters.

TWENTY

Antonia kept as slow a pace as she could. Martin was clearly preoccupied, shoving her along. It was a difficult walk, sometimes nearly a swim as they encountered low-lying areas under several feet of water. She tried to keep her mind from imagining what was waiting for her at the boathouse, but scenarios kept scrolling through her mind anyway. Maybe Gavin had taken control, but Gavin's chances against Leland weren't very good, especially when he had Hector to worry about, too. It struck her then that Gavin was a very brave man indeed to continue his mission in the face of impossible odds. Far safer to hide out, hunker down and wait for rescue.

Her ears kept playing tricks on her. Had she heard the sound of Reuben's footsteps behind them? The engine noise from an incoming chopper? Nerves tingling, she forced herself to keep the panic at bay. *Just keep walking. Wait for an opportunity. Wait, wait, wait.*

Still her mind would not slow. If she died there,

if they all did, who would tell Mia? Hector might somehow escape, and he would find her and Gracie. Your sister drowned on the island, Hector would say. So tragic. Martin was right; no one would be left alive to tell the story.

But would Hector really allow his brother to be murdered? This same man who had helped drag her to shore? She was not sure, even after all that had transpired, what nestled deep in Hector's soul, under the greed and hunger for power.

Maybe you should worry about your own soul. The ocean rolled calmly against the shore, soothing and regular now that the angry storm had departed. A life jacket bobbed in the water, dipping and swirling on the waves. Ironic. What she would have given for a life jacket when Leland left her in the ocean. Salt water stung the cuts on her feet and with the pain came a heavy weight of guilt. Too much of her past few years had been steeped in judgment, in hatred and condemnation. If she had been given only twenty-seven years to live, surely the Lord had not meant for her to waste one moment, let alone month upon month mired down in those emotions? *Forgive me, Lord. Forgive.*

She recalled the look of pain on Reuben's face when he toppled backward into the river. His eyes had not been on his own wound, but on her face, as if he wanted his last sight on this earth to be of her. She'd been wrong to nurse the anger, to stoke the fire of her hurts that crippled her spirit. Every moment wasted in anger was an affront to the One who'd given her life. Too late, the wind seemed to whisper.

Tears threatened and she swallowed hard. "He's okay," she muttered savagely. "He's got to be okay." They skirted another flooded section of trail and pushed instead through the sea grass and down into the sandy sweep of ground that was soggy but passable. Great mountains of kelp had been disgorged on the shore and the seabirds were making use of the opportunity to scavenge for fish forced into the shallower water. Wreckage dotted the sand, piled into strange sculptures. She stumbled over a partially covered pipe. While down on one knee she palmed a scoop full of sand and put it in her pocket. Sand against the enemy? Well, David used a handful of rocks, didn't he?

Martin stopped at the approach to the boathouse, pulling her into the trees as he scoped out the structure. There had been some damage, she noted. The roof was partially ripped off the top story, but the upper level was still intact. The lower story housed the three gaps where boats would be secured, and they appeared to be empty. As far as that went, there were no signs of life or movement from the boathouse whatsoever. The stillness pricked up the tiny hairs on the back of her neck.

"See?" she said. "No skimmer. It's gone. He's gone and left you here."

"Shut up," he said.

They crouched there until her knees began to ache, the mosquitos buzzing down to feed on her tired flesh. Reuben always joked that when the world was destroyed, mosquitos would be the last living creatures standing. She shoved down the wave of tenderness and grief the memory churned up. She fingered the sand in her pocket, but he was so close, an eyeful of grit would only stop him for a minute, maybe less.

"There," Martin cried, stabbing a finger at the remnants of a rickety dock some fifty yards from the boathouse. "The skimmer's tied there neat as you please. Leland's still here."

Antonia did not know what to make of it, or how to use the information to her advantage. "Why is it tied there instead of the boathouse?"

Martin shook his head. "Dunno. I'm going to check it out. You stay here."

Her stomach tensed. Now was her opportunity. Martin took a few cautious steps toward the dock. She readied herself to run as fast as she could manage into the trees. One more step. As soon as he took one more step away she'd take off.

He stopped as if he'd suddenly changed his mind. Her stomach dropped as he returned to her and dragged her close to a tree, yanking her arms around it and fastening her wrists together with his belt. "Just in case you get any ideas, honey," he said, so close she could feel his sour breath on her face.

"I won't..." she started to plead, but he wasn't listening. Tightening the belt, he returned to his wary approach toward the skimmer.

She yanked at the bonds, succeeding only in bringing a shower of water from the wet leaves down on her head. The tree was fairly smooth, but she started sawing her wrists back and forth against it anyway, hoping the bark would begin to wear away the strap of the belt. Out of the corner of her eye she watched Martin approaching the dock. She did not know nor did she care how that skimmer came to be tied on that weathered strip of wood, but she knew she only had a few moments before he checked it out and returned.

"Come on, come on," she whispered impatiently, feeling the belt scratching into her wrists.

Martin made it onto the planked walkway, past tall patches of oat grass. The skimmer was tied to the end, bobbing gently in the calm water. One spot of the belt wore away. Breath exploding, Antonia worked even harder, feeling her palms grow slippery with blood from her chafed wrists. A moment more. She needed only a fraction of a minute of sustained effort to free herself.

Martin drew even with the skimmer, peering down into the vessel. "There's blood in here," she thought he said.

Blood? Maybe she'd misheard over the rolling waves. She sawed harder at the restraint, her nerves burning.

He pulled at something she could not make out.

"Radio's still busted," he yowled. "Lying little…"

She pulled as hard as she could and felt the belt giving slightly.

Martin looked over and his eyes widened. He moved to step over the edge of the boat and back onto the dock.

Something erupted from below in a shower of water. As she struggled to make out what was happening, she felt a hand grasp her shoulder, the fingers long and cold.

Reuben used every bit of momentum he could muster as he exploded from the water and yanked Martin downward. Caught completely off guard, the man went over face-first into the shallows. The impact of the body slamming into the surface nearly took Reuben off his feet. It wasn't a planned effort, and he hadn't time to consider all the variables. After they'd caught sight of Martin leading Antonia toward the boathouse, they'd just made it in time to secure the boat to the dock and hide before he arrived. He'd hoped Martin would bring Antonia with him to investigate, but he'd tied her up instead. Tied her like an animal. He'd pay for that choice, Reuben had decided.

Catching Martin completely by surprise should have been the end of it. Get him bound and out of the picture quickly, but each movement sent ripples of pain through Reuben's side as he struggled to get his arms around Martin's neck. Martin had weathered the storm better, and his strength seemed undiminished as he fought back, flailing punches at Reuben, who dodged as best he could.

Salt water stung his eyes as Martin landed a punch that caught Reuben in the ribs. The pain blurred his vision and left him unable to suck in a breath. He stumbled backward and nearly went down.

"Shoulda shot you when I had the chance," Martin grunted.

Reuben kept his footing and somehow got his fists up again, fighting through the red wall of pain. "Guess so," Reuben managed. *Think it through, Reuben. You're not stronger than he is. You have to be smarter.* He waited, like Hector had taught him, until the split second after Martin drew back a fraction, telegraphing his intentions. He was going to go for a punishing low swing, probably seeking Reuben's injury again. At the last moment after the blow was launched, Reuben jerked to the side and swept his foot out in a wide arc, knocking Martin's feet out from under him and letting his momentum carry him to the water.

Just as Martin struggled to his feet again, Silvio emerged, oar in hand, and brought it down on the man's skull, the thwack sounding dull and flat. Martin crumpled forward into the water, unconscious. Limbs heavy with fatigue, Reuben flipped him onto his back to keep him from drowning. He looked up at Silvio, panting.

"You could have used the oar a little earlier."

Silvio shrugged. "You were doin' okay, and I had to make sure Paula was hidden."

Reuben moved slowly toward the bank, where Silvio dragged Martin out of the water and rolled him none too gently into the shrubs. "He's gonna wake up a couple of pints short of blood due to the mosquitos." Silvio smiled. "Unless his blood is too foul even for them."

Movement from the trees brought their conversation to a halt.

Through the water coursing down his face, Reuben saw Leland, his hand wrapped in Antonia's hair, running with her toward the boathouse.

"Nee," Reuben shouted. He sprinted toward her, but Leland had a head start. The roar of a helicopter hardly registered as he watched Leland disappear into the lower floor of the cavernous boathouse.

He turned back to Silvio, whose stricken gaze alternated between the boathouse and the helicopter, which was working its way to the far side of the island. "Get Paula. Take the skimmer and go signal them."

"Not gonna do it," Silvio said softly.

Reuben gripped Silvio's shoulders and locked eyes with him. "We need help. You've got to go get it because I'm not leaving her."

"She's hurt you, abandoned you," Silvio said. "You gonna risk your life for her again?"

Reuben could not remember in that moment a single hurt, one disappointment, the tiniest recollection of past pain. His heart and brain were filled only with the precious, the jewellike memories of a love so pure it hurt and a spirit so cleaved to his own that he would not be whole without it.

"I'm going to save her," Reuben said, feeling something strong and sure take the place of the physical pain that wracked his body. He did not know how, but certainty rang through him like the thunder of the waves.

Silvio cocked his head and smiled at Reuben. "I wouldn't have expected any other answer."

Reuben allowed himself to be pulled into a fierce hug and then Silvio was gone to retrieve Paula. He straightened as best he could and marched toward the boathouse. There was no need for stealth, as Leland had already seen what transpired with Martin and the skimmer. He made his way up the path to the lower level and onto the small platform, letting himself into the cavernous underbelly. It was dark, and he blinked as his eyes adjusted. The risen water had topped the platforms that would normally provide docks for the boats to be tied, but it had receded until it was now a few inches below the bloated wood. The beams that held up the roof were blackened with water but still whole and strong. He thought ruefully that his mother would be proud. He took courage from those sturdy beams as he approached the wooden steps to the upper floor.

The bottom step was slick and his feet skidded a bit. He wondered what had happened to Gavin. To his brother. The boards creaked and groaned under his weight. The steps led to a solid platform, a space piled with boxes and opening onto two small rooms that served as more storage and a tiny office space for managing the paddleboat rentals that were so popular when times were better.

Antonia sat on a metal folding chair, hands in her lap, her look a mixture of fear and defiance. Leland stood next to her, a gun held casually in his hand, as if it were nothing more than a TV remote. Her eyes locked on him and something exquisite rippled through those fine features. One tear, glittering and pure, slid down her cheek. He knew that tear was for him.

"Welcome to the boathouse," Leland said. "Did you kill him?"

It took Reuben a moment to realize Leland was speaking about Martin. "No, he's alive."

Leland nodded. "And Granny and Grandpa? What's become of them?"

"They are on their way to flag down the coast

guard." Reuben watched Leland's eyes for some sign of anxiety, but he showed none.

"It's all right," Leland said, almost as if he were speaking to himself. "I've got someone coming to pick me up. Small boat can outrun the coast guard. That's why we love this island so much, isn't it?" He wiggled a small cell phone. "Phones are back up, did you know that? The storm has passed, the clouds have parted and all is right with the world."

Reuben looked at Antonia, calculating the distance and time it would take to reach her. He was not faster than a bullet. "Where's my brother?" he said.

"Put him in the storage room. Didn't give me much of a fight. Going to take him with me when I leave so he can sign the island over to Garza."

"He won't sign," Reuben said.

"Yes, he will. He'll be put out that I murdered his brother, but he'll sign. He's got a kid and an ex-wife to think about after all. How old is the kid, anyway? Two? Three? A real cutie, I'm sure."

Antonia started to stand, rage in her eyes, but Leland pushed her back down. "Stay there, *señorita*. It will be easier for all of us." He cocked his head and fingered her hair. "I just have to know. How did you manage to not drown? No one could have stayed afloat in that storm."

Antonia jerked her head away.

"Not going to tell me? All right," he said with a

sigh. "It will be one of those mysteries you take to the grave."

Reuben's pulse thundered. "The cops are going to know everything. You're caught."

Leland laughed. "Such a naive boy. I'm going to become someone else. Garza will set me up in Mexico maybe or the tropics. I'm still useful to him, being so skilled and all." He called loudly over his shoulder. "Hector, come out here, please."

The door remained closed. Leland sighed and fired a round into the rafters just above the door. Antonia screamed as the sound echoed through the space. Reuben lurched toward Leland, but he stopped him by aiming the gun at Antonia and waggling a finger.

"Come on out, Hector," Leland shouted, "or the next one goes through the door."

Reuben saw his brother emerge from the storage room, shoulders slumped. His eyes were smudged with shadows, bruises darkening his skin and a smear of dried blood on his chin. Face slack with shock, he looked at Antonia and then his brother.

"I'm sorry," he said. "I never meant for any of this to happen. I'd hoped to give you time to get away."

"I'm sure he knows that," Leland said. "Very touching, the brotherly bond and all that. I simply wanted you to see me kill these two so you'll remember how it looked and how they sounded, et cetera. Fix it in your memory, Hector, and keep it there so if you're tempted to change your mind about signing over Isla or some such foolishness, you can stroll down memory lane and imagine how a bullet will impact a small child."

"You don't need to kill them," Hector blurted out. "My brother will hand it over now, won't you?" Hector's tone was pleading. "You can stop all this, Reuben."

Reuben felt a mixture of disgust and compassion. "Yes," he said, gaze on his brother. "Leland, you don't have to kill anyone."

Leland laughed. "I'm not sure you're right." He spoke to Hector as if they were the only people in the room. "These two—" he gestured the gun at Reuben and Antonia "—they seem to have that fire in the belly, a certain antiquated desire to cling to the moral high ground, a quality that you don't have, Hector. I can't see them blithely going along with Mr. Garza and being the quiet little church mice for the foreseeable future. They have that look in their eyes that spells trouble."

Hector shook his head. "Don't kill them. They haven't done anything wrong."

"Mmm." Leland pulled out his cell phone and checked the screen. "Ah. My ride is here. Hector, head downstairs, please." When Hector didn't move, Leland fired another shot into the rafters, which made Antonia scream again and his brother cringe. Hector took several slow, shuffling steps away.

"It's been lovely chatting with you, but my schedule is full. Gentlemen first." He swiveled the gun at Reuben and pulled the trigger.

TWENTY-ONE

Antonia threw her handful of sand just as Leland's finger depressed the trigger. At the same time, Reuben launched himself at Leland, who jerked backward instinctively as the sand pricked his eyes, clawing at his face.

She picked up the chair and brought it down on Leland's back with all the strength she possessed as he rolled on top of Reuben. The metal impacted Leland's skull with a thwack and sent the gun flying under a pile of boxes. Leland went limp. She helped Reuben get slowly to his feet, tears crowding her vision, mind disbelieving the events her eyes had just witnessed.

After one tight hug, he grabbed her hand and pulled her away. They met Hector at the stairs. "We have to get out of here before his men arrive," Hector said.

Feet echoing on the steep steps, they made their way quickly. From upstairs they heard a groan as

Leland fought his way back to consciousness. Antonia's skin prickled in panic.

They plunged down to the landing, and she noticed that Reuben stumbled slightly, whether from haste or blood loss she was not sure. They headed for the exit just as a boat motored into the structure. As the man blinked to adjust to the darkness, the three shrank back into the shadows, but they were not quick enough. The boat captain pulled a weapon from his belt and began firing, the shots exploding in ear splitting percussions all around them, drilling deep tunnels into the wood siding.

There was no place to hide, no trace of cover. Splinters careened above their heads as they took the only chance open to them and plunged feetfirst into the water. Antonia felt Hector and Reuben punch through the surface a split second after she did. They slid under the planked dock and came up for air. Her head bumped the wood. There were only a few inches between the waterline and the underside of the dock. She sucked as much oxygen as she could in that tiny, precious gap.

"Get out to the ocean," Reuben breathed next to her. "We're easy targets here."

Shots cut into the wood above them as the shooter raked the slip with bullets. They went under again, as deep as they could, but Antonia could still feel bullets chugging through the water near her shoulders and head. She pressed in the direction she figured led to the open ocean, but a second spray of bullets made them again take cover under the other platform. The shooter had leaped from the boat and run to the end of the dock, firing at close range into the water, here, there, at every swirl or splash, determined to find his target in spite of the darkness.

Reuben shoved Antonia behind him and backed them as far away from the shooter as he could. She rested her cheek against his shoulder, panting. The boathouse went so quiet their own harsh breathing sounded loud. She bit her lip between her teeth. A flash of movement from above revealed the boat captain bent over, peering underneath the planking of the dock right next to them. His feet made the boards creak and moan as he peered into the water, inch by meticulous inch.

Leland came down the stairs, a look of fury on his face, hair damp with blood. He gestured wildly with the gun and began his own perusal of the farthest dock, shooting methodically into the wood every few inches. There was no emotion on his face except pure, unadulterated rage, and she knew this time he would kill them on sight.

She held Reuben around the shoulders, knowing that he was frantically trying to formulate some means of escape. It was only a matter of minutes before they were discovered. They had to buy time, to live, until the coast guard arrived or Gavin managed to get some reinforcements there to help them.

Hector crouched near enough that his shoulder touched hers. His lips were moving, but she could not hear any words. He looked small and scared, and hopeless.

Leland shouted loud enough for her to hear his every syllable as he paced the dock.

"I am going to kill you all. Do you hear me?" he roared. "All of you."

Something moved next to her and she almost screamed. Before she could make sense of what she was seeing, Hector dove low and swam out into the open water between the slips.

"No!" Reuben lunged for him, but Hector was away before he could catch hold. Reuben's profile was etched in anguish as his brother swam into the line of fire. She understood then. Hector was providing them a distraction, a precious moment to swim away undetected.

She'd thought him a coward. She'd believed he was purely selfish, but in this final act of heroism, he'd proven her wrong.

A shudder went through Reuben. It was as if she could sense his heart breaking inside his body. Tension, grief, outrage or maybe some other emotion balled the muscles in his back, and she felt a deep quiver run through him before he began to move. He would not let his brother's sacrifice go to waste. He pulled her toward the opening, and after one breath they plunged as deep as they could before striking out for the ocean. Her sodden clothes pulled her back, tired muscles and exhaustion working against her as they kicked hard, scooping their way through the shadowed black water toward the brilliant blue sea.

Had she heard more shots? Was there shouting? She could not be sure over the pounding of her pulse as her body screamed for oxygen. A few more strokes and she felt the warmth of the sunlight-kissed water against her fingertips. Another two kicks and she broke to the surface, sucking in desperate lungfuls of sweet air. She was several yards out of the boathouse, she realized, the shore glittering invitingly to her right, sun dazzling her eyes.

Treading water she called to Reuben. "Come on." When she received no reply she began to turn in slow circles, frantic energy pooling in her stomach. Finally, his head broke the surface, but his eyes were half closed and face pale as the Florida sand.

She reached him in a few hard strokes, moving behind him and supporting his head and shoulders. "It's all right," she whispered. "We'll make it."

She towed him toward shore, all the while eyeing the boathouse. The motor sound ignited a fresh terror inside her. The boat broke out of the shadows, two figures aboard. It didn't take them long, only seconds really, before they spotted Antonia and Reuben. Antonia squeezed Reuben to her chest and kicked for all she was worth toward the shore.

* * *

They were not going to make it, not this way. Frustration and anger tainted every breath as Reuben tried to kick and help Antonia get them to shore. He knew the puffs of blood billowing in the water were from his stab wound, but he felt no pain, not in his body anyway. He wondered if Hector had. He remembered the swimming races they'd conducted as kids, the staying-underwater competitions that Hector won every time to Reuben's chagrin. Hector was not content to lose, but he had this time. He'd lost so Reuben and Antonia could live.

The thought gave him a ripple of energy, and he flipped over on his stomach. Antonia gave him a surprised look. "Okay?"

"Okay. Go, go," he gasped, putting a hand on her back and shoving her through the water.

Without another word they swam as hard as they could for shore. He tried to let his good arm do most of the work, but every motion reminded him the right side of his body was not working properly. The muscles seemed deadened, as if they belonged to someone else.

He heard the boat draw closer and closer, but the water underneath him was shallowing out, warming as they reached the shore. Bullets burst through the foaming waves.

Stroke, kick, breathe. His body was fueled now on one ferocious determination. He would not let

Leland take her life. They would not steal away the single precious gift in his possession like they had taken his brother and threatened to do with Gracie. Sprays of water splashed his face as Leland continued to fire. Stroke, kick, breathe. Antonia kept darting looks over her shoulder to make sure he was still following.

"Just go," he shouted. "Don't wait for me."

She pressed on until he saw her scramble to her feet and reel onto the shore like a wave coming home to the sand.

His heart leaped. She'd made it. She'd made it. His feet found purchase on the ground and he staggered in her direction, but his legs would no longer hold him. He felt himself falling, the shore reaching up to receive him. Then she was there, tugging on his arm.

"Come on, Reuben. Come on," she pleaded. She grabbed him under the arms and attempted to drag him along the sand, but the slope was steep and he outweighed her.

He tried to get his knees underneath him with no success. The terrible numbness seemed to have crept from his wound through the rest of his torso, his legs, his arms, leaving them stiff and numb. She knelt next to him, staring into his face. "Please," she whispered, water trailing down her long hair and onto his chest.

"Nee, you've got to go. Get to the trees. Now."

"I'm not leaving you."

He closed his eyes for a moment, feeling the exquisite brush of joy against his soul. Somewhere under all the pain, she still felt something for him. "I've lost my brother and Isla. Don't let that be for nothing. Go, go now."

Her black eyes were huge, glimmering with helplessness and something else. He reached up to stroke her cheek. "There's that pilgrim soul again."

She settled next to him, hand brushing the sand from his face. The boat engine was loud now. He struggled to sit up and saw that the vessel was a mere six feet from shore. Leland's white teeth shone as he grinned and brought the gun up into firing position.

Reuben summoned his last bit of strength and shoved her behind him. At least he could offer her some small protection with his own body. As he braced for the bullets, his senses were confused by the heavy chop of rotors that whirled the sand into a frenzy. It was a coast guard helicopter. Two boats sped into view seemingly out of nowhere, police sirens competing with the helicopter noise, armed officers shouting commands.

For an endless moment, Leland appeared to be considering. Then his arms went up in a gesture of surrender along with his companion's. One of the police boats pulled close to shore and disgorged a man who ran up the beach.

Gavin dropped down next to him. His shoulder was bandaged, arm secured in a sling. He gave Reuben the once-over and spoke quietly into his radio, summoning medical help, Reuben imagined.

"Well, Mr. Sandoval, it seems you have managed to survive. Silvio said things had gotten a bit tense around here. So much for a tropical island getaway."

Reuben fought to keep his eyes open. "Thought you were going to arrest Leland at the boathouse."

"Hector got away from me and went charging on in. My phone came back online so I called in the troops and went to meet them. No offense, but your brother is a real piece of work."

The pain knifed through him again. He tried to talk, but only a sigh came out.

"Hector swam out to Leland," Antonia explained. "To give us time to escape." She smoothed the hair out of Reuben's eyes, fingers cool and gentle against his skin.

"Oh, was that the truth?" Gavin raised an eyebrow. "I thought he was embellishing."

Reuben jerked. "He's okay? You talked to him?"

"Sure. He managed to get out of it with a couple of superficial wounds. We picked him up just before we busted Leland—and saved you two, I might add."

Reuben wanted to shout, to hug the skinny DEA agent, whose profile began to swim before his eyes. "My brother is alive."

"Yep. Alive and going to prison, but he says he's

okay with that. Even offered up his involvement in the drug deal a few years back. He's going to prison, like I said, but his cooperation will help."

A medic arrived and began to peel back the remains of Reuben's tattered shirt to assess the damage, followed by another with a stretcher. Reuben lay in a helpless lump as they ministered to him. He could not feel the pressure of their hands and soon even their calm, measured voices blurred into the background. The only thing his senses would hold on to was Antonia's black eyes, staring into his, her lips moving in words he could not hear, stroking his forehead with fingers he could not feel.

But those eyes…

They were alive, and vibrant. He wanted to put his hand out and feel that satin cheek, to tell her one more time that he was the man who loved the pilgrim soul in her, who savored the shadows of her changing face.

We've made it through the storm, he wanted to say. His mother had been right. There was no storm too big for God.

Instead he stared into her eyes until the darkness crept into his own.

Minutes ticked into days. Antonia took turns pacing around the joyless hospital waiting room, alternating paths with Silvio and Paula. Interrupting the pacing were interviews with the police, rehashing every detail from her reckless swim into the ocean with the man on the Jet Ski, to the horrifying conclusion in the boathouse. She'd gone over an edited version with her sister, Mia, as soon as she'd been able to get hold of a borrowed phone. The phone buzzed again and Antonia picked it up.

"Is Reuben okay?" Mia asked.

"They're still waiting to see if the fever breaks. The infection is a nasty one."

"I'm coming home."

Antonia sucked in a breath. "Really? When?"

"Tomorrow. I've got enough for the red-eye. I need to—" Her voice broke off and after a steadying breath she continued, "I need to thank Reuben personally for saving your life."

Antonia sighed. "Reuben will be overjoyed to see Gracie." She paused. "What are you thinking about? Hector?"

Mia was silent for a moment. "He did terrible things, but knowing what happened, I think he really does love Gracie. When she's old enough, I'll make sure she knows her father made mistakes but he tried to do the right thing in the end. We'll play it by ear when he gets out of prison." Another pause. "So what about you and Reuben? Where do things stand with the two of you?"

Where did they stand? She was filled with a deep and overwhelming gratitude that God had spared his life and hers, but her heart was such a jumble of emotion she could not discern what was posttraumatic shock and what was real. "I don't know."

They ended the conversation with information about flights and preparations for Mia and Gracie to return to the old house. There would need to be cleaning done and supplies purchased for the little girl, storm damage seen to. It was a relief to put her mind to the prosaic details of daily living.

She disconnected and let the quiet of the waiting room soothe her mind. Silvio and Paula had gone to stay with relatives, who graciously agreed to accept Charley the cat, also. At that moment, they were away for a short time, seeing to the details. A nurse exited Reuben's room and gave her a wide smile.

"Fever's broken," she said triumphantly. "He's going to be right as rain. Might even get to go home soon."

Antonia closed her eyes, dizzy with relief.

"You can go in and see him now," she said.

Antonia's heart raced and her hands went cold. Now that he was safe, his life restored, she was left with the question Mia had raised. Pulse fluttering in her throat, she walked slowly into his room. He was asleep, face scratched and bruised, still pale, but with a flush of normal color returning.

She leaned over the bed and studied him. Suddenly, all the emotions came crashing in, like the crushing waves of a hurricane, firing memories both happy and horrifying into her mind. Their life, their love, had exploded into shards of debris that presented itself to her now at such lightning-quick speeds her heart could not figure out how to respond.

She leaned down and kissed him on the mouth, pressed her forehead to his and ran from the room.

Two days after his release from the hospital, Reuben stepped over the broken branches of his orange trees, savoring the cool air on his face. They'd been denuded of their leaves and though some were still standing like stalwart soldiers amidst the wreckage, the roots of the old Valencia poked from the earth, defeated.

It was painful to see the seasoned trees, which had been so productive and vibrant, reduced to trash. *It's all right,* he thought. *I'm not defeated.*

With only a small twinge of pain from his ribs, he bent and dug a handful of earth, raising it to his nose and inhaling deeply the earthy scent of promise. He would rebuild the orchard and coax life from the ground again, with God's help. The air would be filled with the perfumed blossoms and bejeweled with the lush color of oranges once more. The road would be hard and expensive, but he would travel it, somehow.

Optimism fought with another emotion. His gaze

wandered to the blue sky, and he wondered where Antonia had gone. He did not blame her for taking off. His choices and those of his brother almost got her killed. She'd probably fled from the hospital as soon as she was able, maybe even left Florida altogether, and that would be justifiable.

He flung the soil to the ground and tried to figure out where to start. He was piling the broken branches as best he could into an enormous mound when Antonia appeared underneath the trees, just as if she were part of the orchard itself. The sun glossed her dark hair and pulled at the edges of her yellow dress.

He was unable to speak.

"Hi, Reuben," she said.

He came close slowly, tentatively, afraid that she might run or disappear somehow, evaporate like the clouds. "Antonia. How...how are you?"

"Shouldn't I be asking you that?"

He shrugged. "Just sore. It will take me a while to get back to full steam."

She raised an eyebrow. "And you figured some manual labor would speed things along?"

He laughed. "Hard work is good for the soul."

"Then you have a soul bigger than most," she said before her face grew serious. "What did you decide to do? About Isla, I mean?"

"I'm giving it up, but not to Garza. Deeding the

land to the nature conservancy. No more hotels for me."

"How does that feel?" she asked softly, gathering her windblown hair. "Giving up your mother's dream?"

"I thought it would be devastating, but it hasn't been that way. My mother's real dream was for us to live an honest life. And I'm going to do that, here in my orchard. Hector can join me someday if he wants to." He wondered if the mention of his brother's name would upset her.

"Hector turned out to have some of those honest qualities after all."

"Too bad he didn't display them sooner," Reuben said with a sigh. "It would have prevented a lot of heartache, but that's between him and God."

"You can't save anybody, can you?"

"Nope. That's His job, but I forgot that for a while."

She nodded. For a few moments they were silent, listening to the rustling leaves. "I know it's rude and all, but I brought an uninvited guest."

"Who?"

Gracie and Mia walked up the gravel road. When Gracie saw Reuben, she broke from her mother's hand and trotted on chubby legs as fast as she could.

"Uncle Booben!" she shouted.

He swept her into a hug and clung to her, his heart nearly exploding, throat thick. "Gracie, I've missed you. I love you so much."

Gracie put her small hand on Reuben's cheek and patted gently. "I miss you, too, Uncle Booben." She put a tiny fingertip on the scratch bisecting Reuben's forehead. "You got hurt." She looked at him closer. "And skinny."

"And you got even more gorgeous since I saw you last. Did you grow a couple of feet?" He swung her around in circles until they were both breathless and dizzy, before he put her down.

"Come here, Gracie," Mia said. "Hold Mama's hand and we'll go see if the playhouse Uncle Booben made for you is still standing." She looked at Reuben and took a deep breath. "Thank you for saving my sister. I was wrong to take Gracie from you. I'm truly sorry."

He opened his mouth to answer, to apologize again for his brother, for all that had transpired, but before he could summon up the words, she'd turned and walked away through the trees with Gracie.

Reuben fought for composure as Antonia came near. "I thought…" He cleared his throat. "Thank you. I will never let anything happen to Gracie."

She took his hand then. "She's going to grow up better having Uncle Booben in her life."

He sighed. "I hope so."

Antonia raised his hand and brushed his fingers to her lips, sending tingles spiraling through his body.

"Back on the island," she said, "when I thought I was going to die, I realized how much of my life was spent in anger and blame. I decided that was not what God meant for me, for my life. That's not why He let me survive the storm, so I could go back to holding on to past hurts."

He could not help it. He pulled her close, close enough that he could smell her sun-warmed hair and feel the curve of her body next to his. "Nee, I'm sorry for..."

With a trembling finger, she quieted him with a touch to his mouth. "I know. You told me you're sorry, and so am I. We made mistakes, both of us, and that's done." Her hands fell to his shirtfront and she held them there. He knew she must be able to feel the wild beating of his heart. Something hopeful, joyful, tender lifted inside his soul.

"I'm going to be a farmer, Nee, not a resort owner. Just a simple farmer because that's what God made me to be."

Cocking her head she smiled. "There's nothing simple about you, Reuben."

"I could say the same about you." He stroked her hair. "You are wild and compassionate, beautiful because of what you've been through." She shivered in his arms and he ran his palms over her shoulders, strong and soft at the same time. "I would do anything for you, go anywhere because I love you." He offered up the words, bare and vulnerable, delicate as an orange blossom. "I'll always love you."

Tears glistened in her eyes. "You won't have to go

anywhere. You'll stay here, on your farm, and we'll build it again, together."

Together. His friend, his love, the most precious creation he had ever been blessed to see. Reuben and Antonia. Together.

"Can this be real?" he whispered, pressing kisses on her temple, her cheeks, her neck.

"Yes, Reuben, it's real," she murmured back, raising her mouth and joining her life to his with a long, slow kiss. "I love you."

He let the joy shudder through him, the storm of emotion blowing away the past until nothing remained but the sun-kissed future that they would face.

Together.

* * * * *

Dear Reader,

As I put the finishing touches on this book, the massive cleanup continues in the wake of Hurricane Sandy, which battered the eastern United States in October 2012. Sandy left dozens dead, thousands homeless and millions without power. It was a hurricane, like many that went before it, that left widespread despair in its wake. Hurricanes, like earthquakes and floods and all manner of natural disasters, remind us how very fragile we are, powerless to control the world around us, at the mercy of whatever nature dishes out.

Even as the reconstruction continues, we know there will be other disasters to follow. There will be another Sandy, or Isaac, or Charley, storms that will visit us in the guise of illness, financial hardship, death of a spouse or child, broken relationships. We know we will face our own personal storms on this dark and dangerous planet. So where do we find comfort? In the knowledge that this world is not the end, and even through the disasters, God is in control. He is preparing us for our journey home and most of all, He sent His beloved Son to walk with us through this life, a precious comfort, a harbor in the storm. I recently came across this quote from Pope John Paul II that spoke more eloquently than I ever could. I hope it blesses you today as much as it did me. "Do not abandon yourselves to despair. We are the Easter people, and Hallelujah is our song."

I am grateful that you spent some of your precious time reading this story. I would love to hear from you via my website at www.danamentink.com. If you prefer to correspond by letter, my physical address is Dana Mentink, P.O. Box 3168, San Ramon, CA 94583. God bless!

Dana Mentink

Questions for Discussion

1. What do you think is Reuben's real motivation for trying to keep Isla afloat?

2. Antonia finds beauty in the broken junonia shell. Are there things in our lives that become more beautiful when they are subject to trials? Explain.

3. Is Reuben's faith in his brother wise or foolish? Have you ever had to defend a family member accused of wrongdoing? How did you handle it?

4. Reuben says, "You can't force someone to love you." How does the Bible define love? Share some examples.

5. Reuben wonders who the real Hector is. Is it possible that Hector is both a devoted father and a criminal?

6. Are all people deserving of forgiveness? What does God say on the subject?

7. Hector is addicted to the power that comes with wealth. Why do some people crave positions of power in our society? What does God tell us we should crave instead?

8. Do you believe that no storm is too big for God? What storms has He helped you through in your life?

9. Orange growing is Reuben's real passion. He believes God gifted him especially to do that work. What do you feel God gifted you to do?

10. Have you ever stopped praying for something because you lost hope that God would answer? How can we come to terms with unanswered prayers?

11. Judgment is God's department. Why do we so often slip into making judgments about others? What is the cure for this problem?

12. Leland is a psychopath, devoid of normal human emotion. What conditions do you think produce such a person? What can society do to deal with such a threat?

13. Antonia is saddened by the ruined plover eggs that never became what they were meant to be. How does God comfort us when someone is taken young, before they can realize their true potential?

14. Since God is the only one who saves souls, what is our call as Christians in this world?

15. The power of a hurricane is mighty indeed. Have you ever experienced such a storm? Share about your experiences.

LARGER-PRINT BOOKS!

GET 2 FREE LARGER-PRINT NOVELS PLUS 2 FREE MYSTERY GIFTS

Love Inspired®
SUSPENSE
RIVETING INSPIRATIONAL ROMANCE

Larger-print novels are now available...

YES! Please send me 2 FREE LARGER-PRINT Love Inspired® Suspense novels and my 2 FREE mystery gifts (gifts are worth about $10). After receiving them, if I don't wish to receive any more books, I can return the shipping statement marked "cancel." If I don't cancel, I will receive 4 brand-new novels every month and be billed just $5.24 per book in the U.S. or $5.74 per book in Canada. That's a savings of at least 23% off the cover price. It's quite a bargain! Shipping and handling is just 50¢ per book in the U.S. and 75¢ per book in Canada.* I understand that accepting the 2 free books and gifts places me under no obligation to buy anything. I can always return a shipment and cancel at any time. Even if I never buy another book, the two free books and gifts are mine to keep forever.

110/310 IDN F5CC

Name	(PLEASE PRINT)
Address	Apt. #
City	State/Prov.	Zip/Postal Code

Signature (if under 18, a parent or guardian must sign)

Mail to the **Harlequin® Reader Service:**
IN U.S.A.: P.O. Box 1867, Buffalo, NY 14240-1867
IN CANADA: P.O. Box 609, Fort Erie, Ontario L2A 5X3

**Are you a current subscriber to Love Inspired Suspense books
and want to receive the larger-print edition?
Call 1-800-873-8635 or visit www.ReaderService.com.**

* Terms and prices subject to change without notice. Prices do not include applicable taxes. Sales tax applicable in N.Y. Canadian residents will be charged applicable taxes. Offer not valid in Quebec. This offer is limited to one order per household. Not valid for current subscribers to Love Inspired Suspense larger-print books. All orders subject to credit approval. Credit or debit balances in a customer's account(s) may be offset by any other outstanding balance owed by or to the customer. Please allow 4 to 6 weeks for delivery. Offer available while quantities last.

Your Privacy—The Harlequin® Reader Service is committed to protecting your privacy. Our Privacy Policy is available online at www.ReaderService.com or upon request from the Harlequin Reader Service.

We make a portion of our mailing list available to reputable third parties that offer products we believe may interest you. If you prefer that we not exchange your name with third parties, or if you wish to clarify or modify your communication preferences, please visit us at www.ReaderService.com/consumerchoice or write to us at Harlequin Reader Service Preference Service, P.O. Box 9062, Buffalo, NY 14269. Include your complete name and address.

LISLPDIR13R

LARGER-PRINT BOOKS!

GET 2 FREE
LARGER-PRINT NOVELS
PLUS 2 FREE
MYSTERY GIFTS

Love Inspired®

Larger-print novels are now available...

ReaderService.com

Manage your account online!

- Review your order history
- Manage your payments
- Update your address

*We've designed
the Harlequin® Reader Service
website just for you.*

Enjoy all the features!

- Reader excerpts from any series
- Respond to mailings and
  special monthly offers
- Discover new series available to you
- Browse the Bonus Bucks catalog
- Share your feedback

Visit us at:

ReaderService.com